MW01517348

SWEENEY

ON-THE-FRINGE

Printed in the United States of America
Limited Edition

Designer: Victoria Dalis
Cover Photo: Brian Nevins, bnsrfphoto@yahoo.com
Author's Photo: Elizabeth Woods
Back Cover Photo: Sandra Seitz
Typeface: MetaPlusNormal and Simoncini Garamond text with
    MilkShake display
Printer: Thomson-Shore, Inc.

ACKNOWLEDGEMENTS
An excerpt from chapter 4 first appeared in *The Surfer's Path*, Issue 59.

The poems "From Kid to Consultant," "'The Seed,' Pancho's Dream" and "Contemplating the Penacook Bridge" first appeared in the journal *Entelechy International: A Journal of Contemporary Ideas*, Number 4, 2006.

Loom Press
P.O.Box 1394, Lowell, MA 01853
http://www.loompress.com

for Elizabeth Sokol, suerte y amor.

THANKS TO:

My brother Justin and my mother and father for giving me all of the love and opportunities a person could hope for in a lifetime. Same goes for the rest of my family and old friends I'm unable to include here. Crucial thanks to Paul Marion and Matt Miller for their friendship, poetry and wisdom. Fred Nutter, Tanya Walsh, Otis Horning, Kalimah Salahuddin and Sarah McAdams Corbett were great friends and critics along the way. Sam Bowen, rest in peace, thanks for being the first reader of any version of this story. Thanks to David Reddick, Kent Layton, Lance Stanley, John Downs and the rest of the Cuatro Casas-Boat Ranch crew for sharing. Thanks to Marcelo Luque in Ecuador and Kemp and Ella Aaberg in California. Thanks to Will "The Aluminium Zebra," Scott Rosecrans and Mark Kuzma for your friendship, critiques and all the beers. All of my friends and fellow writers in San Diego: Joe, Teresa, Tim, Sara, Ryan, Tony, Christine, Scott, Cassandra and everyone else (can't fit you all in here, sorry) that gave such great feedback over the years. Harry Polkinhorn's intelligence, humor and guidance were invaluable in helping me find the form and direction for this book. Thank you for being such a great teacher, Harry. Thanks to Richard Boyd, Hal Jaffee and Jerry Farber as well. Sandra Alcosser and Sharon Bryan were encouraging, supportive and helped me to realize the potential of the poems in this piece. Thanks to all the people of Lowell, Massachusetts. As my brother once said, "I wouldn't want to be from anywhere else." Wherever I go in this world, I find I'm in agreement with that sentiment.

Thanks to Trevor Joyce for his translation entitled, The Poems of Sweeney Peregrine. *That book is the original inspiration for this project. I owe a lot to Mr. Joyce. Hope I can find you to get you a copy of this thing! I'm grateful also for the translations and adaptations of Seamus Heaney, T.S. Eliot and Flann O'Brien. It was all inspiring to me. Thanks to MeKeel McBride for her warmth and encouragement many years ago, and Charles Simic for your imagination and the recommendation way back when. Brock Dethier, as well, has been a good friend and great teacher through the years.*

Lastly, I'd like to thank the inimitable, the talented, the poetic, the funny, the gruff, the honest, the blunt, the scholarly and the friendly Glover Davis for teaching me so much in such a short time. It's impossible to for me to describe how valuable my time with you has been (even though I can hear you telling me it's my job as a poet to be able to describe such things). Thank you, Glover, for living a life dedicated to the craft of poetry. I couldn't have done much without your example.

CONTENTS

SWEENEY'S POEMS

This is a book of water. This is a book of meditation. This is a book about one man, Sweeney, whose story runs as deep and as troubled as the water in which, as a surfer, he lives much of his life. We hear about Sweeney through his poetry. We hear about Sweeney through Owen Kivlin, the narrator and guide. Most of all we hear about Sweeney through the people of Seawell. Their Sweeney stories echo those told by villagers about classical heroes of folktales and myths. These were heroes whose abilities and experience stood out from those of other men—heroes such as Beowulf, the poet Orpheus and Ireland's warrior poet Sweeney Peregrine, upon whose tale this book is built.

Dave Robinson's Sweeney is a hero marked by the modern world. Like Eliot's Prufrock he feels the withering stare of conventional society. Like Kesey's Randle Patrick McMurphy, Sweeney's search for answers pushes him past society's boundaries as its trappings attempt to pull him down. Most of all, Sweeney reminds me of Melville's Ishmael. If I could get into Sweeney's head I imagine his thoughts would reflect Ishmael's at the opening of Moby Dick:

> Whenever I find myself growing grim about the mouth; whenever it is a damp, drizzly November in my soul; whenever I find myself involuntarily pausing before coffin warehouses, and bringing up the rear of every funeral I meet; and especially whenever my hypos get such an upper hand of me, that it requires a strong moral principle to prevent me from deliberately stepping into the street, and methodically knocking people's hats off— then, I account it high time to get to sea as soon as I can.

For Sweeney the ocean also seems to ever offer this baptism of healing and nourishment. It is for him both bread and balm.

Yet we may read his poetry, we may hear of his exploits but we never get that naked moment of thought that Ishmael gives us. And as much as I would like to spend some hours in Sweeney's head, that, fortunately, is not the story Robinson has crafted for us here. This is not simply one man's journey among others to find his self. Rather, it is a journey of others to literally and figuratively find Sweeney. And we, the readers, through Robinson's skillful narrative, are as well woven through this experience. The delight of reading this book is that the story reaches into some sense of shared human connection, compelling us to continue searching and holding out hope for Sweeney, for Sweeney's people, for the people in our own lives.

The characters in this story are more central, more alive, than the word "characters" signifies. They are very much Whitman's roughs, those Americans that he heard singing, from the farm to the factory. In this book, the choir sings for Sweeney. They tell his tale because he is the hero they need in a certain time and place and form, whether as the boy naturalist, the baseball player, the surfer, the poet, the matador, the artist, the seeker. But they are more than roughs, more than salty folk satisfied with their lot. They dream and hurt and wish as much as any blood-and-flesh person. And they tell these stories not just to create the myth of Sweeney they need, but because these are their stories as well. They become part of the myth through the telling of it.

And it is this, I think, that is the heart of the book. Sweeney is the stone in the soup, that thing that tricks all the other ingredients together. The care and attention Robinson gives to the voices and lives of these people betrays his love for them in a way that only writing with empathy, not pity, can. He lives with these people in his heart. And here in this slim yet loaded novel he celebrates them. He sings these people. And, to paraphrase Whitman, every atom belonging to them as good belongs to us.

As I reflect on Sweeney and the storytellers of Seawell, I am again brought back to Ishmael. "Yes, as every one knows," says Ishmael, "meditation and water are wedded for ever." Inside these pages there is wisdom and there are waves. Both are powerful. Treacherous. Exhilarating.

Matthew Miller
Exeter, New Hampshire
October, 2 0 0 7

Dave Robinson

SWEENEY
ON-THE-FRINGE

LOOM PRESS
2007
Lowell, Massachusetts

My name is Owen Kivlin; I was once friends with a man named Sweeney, the most memorable person I've met in my lifetime.

A few Seawell locals, most of them several years older than me, swear on their pints of stout that Sweeney lived on a retired fishing trawler—perched on beam-ends, stilts and barrels somewhere in the woods to the right of number six at the Farannan Golf Course. They claim they used to hang out with him in the winter while they were "practicing their drinking" on the course during high school, before they were old enough to get into the bars downtown. These are just a few of the people in Seawell, Sweeney's hometown in Massachusetts, who were eager to tell me about their connection to the man. I have gathered together a dozen or so of these stories in an effort to pass on the legend of Yardbird Sweeney.

I.

Seawell is a harbor/mill town of nearly one-hundred fifty thousand people that sprawls along the banks of the Merrohawke River as it empties into the Atlantic Ocean a couple of hours north of Cape Cod, Massachusetts. The residents are a mix of factory workers, lobstermen, fishermen and a growing population of graduates from Seawell University who commute to Boston daily for their earnings.

Seawell is often referred to as "the armpit of Massachusetts" by the residents of Boston and its suburbs. The departure of the mill industry after World War II, the recession in the '80s, and the depletion of the cod population off The Georgia Bank hit the city hard. The downtown area was rundown, and local business owners steadily lost customers to the homogenized malls popping up just over the border in New Hampshire. During this time, gang violence and drug trafficking became well-publicized problems in Seawell, thereby only adding to the nasty reputation of the city.

Seawell is and always has been decidedly blue-collar, while harboring small enclaves of upper-class businessmen and property owners. Many of them still reside atop the hills in the original mansions built by the mill owners in the 19th century. However, Seawell owes its survival—and recent economic and cultural revival—to the waves of immigrants who continually arrive from their own troubled countries to work in the factories in the city and on the boats off its coastline. First the Irish fled the potato famine and came looking to dig the city's canals, as that was the only work the mill-owning English would allow them to undertake. Eventually the Irish moved up to the factories and the fishing boats and began treating the arriving French Canadians as they had been treated by the English. Later, the French Canadians found the Greeks to be second-class citizens— in turn, the Greeks took their angst out on the Polish. The Polish showed distaste for the Southeast Asians who fled the Khmer Rouge, the Southeast Asians for the African Americans, and so on and so forth through the arrival of the Dominicans who currently feud with the local Puerto Ricans. Lately, we are welcoming as best we can the West Africans who are fleeing political strife, famine and genocide in their own ravaged homelands.

II.

Just like Sweeney, I was born and raised in Seawell. I went to Seawell High School in the downtown area (also known as the Acre), and I experienced firsthand all of the intricacies of the richly diverse populations and cultures present in my home town. I also grew up with my mentor and good friend Sweeney watching out for me—when he was around, that is. And, in a way, Sweeney and I have confided in each other since I was about four or five years old. While rumor, insinuation and speculation form the basis of his local legend, I was fortunate enough to hear many stories directly from the man.

What prompted me to collect these stories was their seeming shelf life. I've found that many of the same tales I heard from Sweeney have been passed on in one form or another among the people of Seawell since my childhood. To this day, many, many people in this city still talk about "that loony guy that lived in the boat out in the woods."

Some people claim to know Sweeney from his drinking and brawling days at The Old Wardin House. Some remember his raw athletic talent—he ran the 110 hurdles in high school in the winter; played catcher and shortstop, and hit clean-up for the varsity baseball team as a sophomore, junior and senior. However, the lure of the ocean and traveling seems to have cut Sweeney's promising baseball career short. Other locals dwell on the fact that he spent some time in Darville Mental Hospital for a serious mental disorder. This illness came not too long after Sweeney had served time at The Merritt House of Corrections for his part in a bar brawl. Those closest to Sweeney speak of his eerie connection to the ocean, though few are fortunate enough to have witnessed his genius in person as he slid across the faces of the waves off Seawell Beach.

The old timers at the bar in the Farannan Golf Course clubhouse called Sweeney "Yardbird." Gerald Francis, a retired fireman and lifetime resident of Seawell, seemed to know Yardbird pretty well from his days at Farannan. Gerald was always more than happy to pass on a story or two about him. Gerald detailed—in a stroke-induced, hoarse whisper—why everyone at the golf course knew Yardbird:

> That kid was always frog huntin' at the pond on nine. All summer long he'd be out there and then after school in the fall, too—year after year. He had eyes like a hawk. You could just yell over to him: 'Yardbird, I lost a Titleist-three to the right on number six, two-hundred-forty-yards out.' And off he'd go, flying across the course and into the woods to find the damn thing. He was a fast little bugger, and he was worth every penny. He was a tough kid with these darting, alert eyes—always muddy and smiling. He'd give you your exact ball, plus two more, then expect you to buy the two other balls for fifty cents each. 'Sundown special,' he'd say with a grin, 'this deal won't be around tomorrow.' Usually, I'd see him outside the pro shop near the end of the day, a smile on his tanned face, with purple stains on his shirt from the grape soda he bought with his hard-earned money.

My father, Patrick Kivlin, and Sweeney also met on that same golf course when Sweeney was around six years old; they remained close as Sweeney made his way to high school and my father finished up college at Seawell State University. My father is almost ten years older than Sweeney and he kept an eye on him as a sort of mentor and friend as they grew up together—much like Sweeney did for me when I was young. The two friends spent their younger years together at Farannan—my father usually caddying and Sweeney usually hunting frogs or lost golf balls. My father agrees with Gerald Francis that no kid could match Sweeney's ability at either pastime. Sweeney and my father drank a lot of that hard-earned grape soda together under the shade of the awning by the pro shop.

But my father points out that this wasn't where they spent all their time in the summer. Neither of them particularly cared for golf, they seemed to like the open, green space the course provided and they also coveted its proximity to the surf spots of Seawell. By working there, so to speak, they both could keep an eye on the surf conditions. Whenever there was a swell in the North Atlantic the two of them surfed in the mornings until the wind turned onshore. They would then stash their boards in the woods, and run all over the golf course for the day. Later, the two would grab their boards from the woods and go back out for a surf in the evening if the wind had died and the ocean had glassed off. Eventually, through their work at Farannan, both had saved up enough money for wetsuits and began surfing together right through the winter.

They were a lot like brothers. My father claims Sweeney was an incredible athlete but, at heart, "He was a traveler, a surfer and a poet." He was such a good writer that my father, with the money he made as an environmental consultant for the state, helped fund some of Sweeney's travels and writings as he got older— hoping that a work of art would come of his many talents. But Sweeney has remained in obscurity as an artist while his reputation as an athlete, wildman and world traveler has persisted and grown—at least locally—after he disappeared.

This book contains the stories Sweeney told in my house for years and years. Some of these are the same that Sweeney took the time to tell me himself when I was just a little boy. Here, however, the people of Seawell speak. Because who better to tell these tales than the people who are keeping the story of Sweeney alive? These are the stories that I miss hearing now that my friend hasn't been heard from or seen for many years.

III.

In addition to the stories, I've gathered a few of the dozens of poems that Sweeney sent me from far-flung corners of the Earth. The poems often arrived scrawled on postcards and scraps of paper mailed to me from Central and South America; other poems arrived carefully scripted on lined paper from places like Vancouver Island, British Columbia; San Clemente, California; and Longville, Minnesota. Sweeney once sent me a poem in blank verse written on the back of a used rifle range target, complete with silhouettes of pigs, ducks, cows and rams! I've yet to figure out the meaning behind that choice of paper; although, chances are just as good that no symbolism was intended.

Unfortunately, I haven't received any poems from Sweeney in approximately five years, since his disappearance in the late '90s. I have placed his best poems, in my opinion, between the stories that make up this book. And now is just as good a time as any to mention the invaluable assistance of Paul Moling—the unofficial poet laureate of Seawell. Paul was tireless in helping me to select the poems best suited to this particular project. We're very excited to share these poems with the larger world. Until now, my family and a few close friends of Sweeney have been the only readers of his work.

I decided to include these poems because I've found they help explain who Sweeney is and how he led his life—in his own words. He often, though not always, wrote about his travels in his poetry—the animals he encountered, the adventures he went on, the jungles and deserts and coasts he explored and sometimes he even wrote of the people he met along the way. There are a gross of tales about Sweeney, but only a small collection of poems in which we hear him speak.

IV.

Yardbird Sweeney isn't some sort of mythical being, in the sense that he's imagined, he was a real guy, born and raised in Seawell like the rest of the people telling these stories. In fact, if he is still alive, he would be 34 years old at the time of the completion of this writing in 2004. But Sweeney's pranks, achievements and eccentricities have taken on a mythical life of their own in the bars and on the beaches of Seawell. It seems important to me to record the talk of his wanderings and the opinions on his whereabouts. It seems vital to me to assemble this portrait of my lost friend. I hope, by the end of this book, you will understand why this project has been my baby. Hopefully you'll know Yardbird Sweeney a little bit better when you have finished reading.

V.

I should leave you with a physical description of Sweeney before you begin. He was six feet tall by most accounts, had dark brown or black hair that was often long and shaggy. He sometimes wore a bushy, full beard that had a hint of red in it. He was muscular but lean, with a lithe, laid-back sort of stride. Those who saw him play baseball and surf all claim he made the difficult act look effortless — he possessed an unassuming grace. And Sweeney's eyes, in my memory, were remarkably clear and a unique shade of green (others say they were blue or even gray). His high school coach, Jorge Mroz, told me the most remarkable thing about Sweeney was his vision. He says Sweeney had the same 20-15 vision as "Teddy Ballgame," a.k.a. Ted Williams, one of the most respected hitters ever to play the game of baseball.

As you can see, Sweeney's reputation has blossomed into a kind of local legend, and it is my hope that this legend may one day become the stuff of myth passed on to the next generation of Seawellians — be they baseball players, fishermen, surfers or factory workers.

What follows is a retelling of Yardbird Sweeney's life in the trees and oceans of New England and his larger world.

—Owen Kivlin

THE SEAWELL DRAWBRIDGE

Rob's cousin, Ricky Spence, was up
for the week from Quincy. Me, James, Rob,
and Stanovich met him one day
at Seawell Beach. We asked about
Quincy and he bragged as we walked
toward the drawbridge that crossed the harbor.

He claimed he "beat the livin' shit
outta Mark Wahlberg, before he
was 'Marky Mark,' before he got
famous." And Stanovich just shook
his head: "Oh, that's bullshit. But I wish
you'd kicked his ass, 'cause Marky Mark
and the Funky Bunch fuckin' suck!"
We laughed, but the kid stuck to his
bold claim: "I shit you not," he said,
"But, whatever. If you bastards don't
believe me, I don't give a fuck."

We liked this kid. We'd only known
him for a couple hours, but his
stories were grade-A bullshit.

The bridge, when we finally got
there, was bumper-to-bumper cars.
A siren cried and faded, bells
rang and the ancient bridgehand swung
the iron gates out with a rumble.
The summer crawl of traffic slowed.
We stood beneath the flashing red
stoplight, and we watched a sailboat
motor and push its way through ebb
tide's steady pull. The wooden boat
was huge, with three masts and furled sails.
The captain was alone on deck,
beside a spotted border collie
on its sealegs. The five of us
stared, and the dog gazed up at the bridge.
The captain stood at the helm, stock-still.
Ricky Spence tapped me on the shoulder:

"You guys usually jump from right
around here?"
                        "Yeah, this is the spot."
"How high's this?"
                        "About forty-five
feet," I said.
                "Ahh, this is a cinch.
We do backflips off double this
height back at the quarries in Quincy."

That snapped Stanovich out of his
trance, gawking at the boat's approach:
"Oh fuck you, Marky Mark. Let's see
a backflip right now."
                        The kid climbed
over the metal rail and looked
down as he leaned forward and held
on like a freckled figurehead:
"OK, Stanovich, you wise ass,
I'll do something good here—for you,
and that damn mutt on deck." The boat
plowed between grey, cement-block pillars
as Ricky Spence jumped up and out.
He threw his head back, yanked his knees
up to his chest, hugged them with both
arms, and he pulled a perfect, slow
full gainer. He uncoiled his tuck,
pointed his feet, crossed his left arm
over his farmer-tanned, white chest
and then, strangely, took care to hold
his nose with his right hand. The dog
sprinted to port to bark and growl
as a grinning Ricky Spence appeared
ten feet from the boat's broad, green side.

Stanovich was silent and stunned.
The collie looked back up at us
just as the aft deck slipped between
the pillars of the bridge. We turned
and watched Spence swim for the south shore,
pulled swiftly by the tidal drag.

—Sweeney
  (Postmarked in Mexico, 1989.)

Chapter 1
BACKSTAGE DANCING

I received a phone call from Margaret Tierney, one of Sweeney's mentors and friends as a child. She told me one of her former fourth graders had an experience with Sweeney that might interest me. I interviewed Erin Hamasaki while she was on lunch break at the Bolcain Glen, a gourmet restaurant in Tyngsboro, Massachusetts. At the time of the interview, Erin was seventeen years old, about five-foot-seven, a little on the gangly side, with short-cropped, shining black hair. She came across as a very intelligent girl. Erin was born and raised in the Rathmines section of Seawell, and has become an avid surfer in her own right. At first, she was a little uncomfortable with the tape recorder, but as the interview continued she grew more accustomed to it and seemed to open up to my questions.

So, Erin, nice to meet you.
Umm...hi. Nice to meet you, too.

Erin, I want to ask you a few questions about your experience with Sweeney. I'm getting together a few stories from people who knew him in Seawell.
Well, I guess I didn't really know him, I just...I mean, we just met that one time at Seawell Beach. So, maybe I'm not, like, the right person to interview.

Well, I talked to Margaret Tierney about you and she said you had a really interesting story to tell...
Who's Margaret Tierney? Oh, wait, you mean Ms. Tierney from the Oakland?

Yes, I'm sorry, Ms. Tierney, your fourth grade teacher.
She was my favorite teacher at the Oakland. I love Ms. Tierney!

And she remembers you as one of her favorite students. She told me that you might help me out by telling me your Sweeney story.
Oh, I guess I can tell you what happened. It wasn't any real big deal or anything, but if you need to know...wait, what's this for again?

I'm just putting together a collection of stories about Sweeney. You know, all those stories you always hear about him going crazy and living on the golf course and stuff like that.
Really?! That's cool. He did some pretty cool shit, from what I hear. I mean um, wait. You can't put in the swear words. Can you cut that swear out of there? My mother would kill me if she ever knew I said that.

No problem, I'll get rid of that for you. Don't worry. But can you tell me about the day you saw Sweeney surfing?
Umm, yeah. What do you want me to say?

Just tell me how you met him. Who were you on the beach with?
Well, that's a funny thing. This is another thing that my mother'd kill me for if she knew about it. I was down the beach by myself that day, and I wasn't supposed to be. I was only a kid. I think I was in second grade then. Yeah, I was, because I remember I couldn't wait to go to school the next day and tell Mrs. Brown about surfing, but she was absent that day. I wanted to tell her so bad, too. She was my second-favorite teacher at the Oakland, after Ms. Tierney.

And why were you at the beach by yourself when you were only, what, seven or eight years old?
(Laughs, and blushes a little in embarrassment) I ran away from home.

You ran away from Rathmines, across the whole city, to Seawell Beach?
Yeah, I took the bus. The bus ran near my house on Stevens St. my whole life, and I'd always wanted to take it somewhere, but my mother always drove me everywhere. It's kinda weird, I know, but, umm, I like riding on buses and trains and stuff like that. So I took the bus all the way to downtown and then walked a couple miles out to Seawell Beach.

Your parents still don't know you did this?
(Laughs) No. No way! I told them I was over at the Mahoney's house all afternoon. The Mahoney's lived right down the street, and I was always hanging out with them. My parents didn't even suspect that I was gone *(more laughter, and covers her mouth)*.

OK, so you get to the beach and what do you see?
Well, it was in May or early June, and it was wicked nice out. So I was just sorta wading in the water and watching the waves. It was a weekday, a Wednesday, and we had a half-day at school for some teacher's convention or something stupid like that. Half-days were the best! But they don't have them anymore, except near Thanksgiving and Christmas. Yeah, umm, so I was just wading in the water, up to my ankles, with my shoes off. The water was fuh...umm, the water was wicked cold. I remember that much, because my feet went numb so I started to turn around to walk back up to the warm soft sand and Sweeney was standing up in the soft sand. He sorta scared me, because no one was on the beach at all that day. Like I said, it was a Wednesday and everyone was at work. The beach was totally empty.

Did he say anything to you?
Well, I knew I wasn't supposed to talk to strangers so I didn't want to talk to him. I was trying to ignore him, so I turned back toward the water and I pretended I was looking for shells in the sand. I crouched down and I was picking at the little pieces of shells and crab claws and stuff at the edge of the water. And then he came up to me and he says to me, "How's the water?" He asked me like I was an adult or something! I thought he was gonna ask me what I was doing down there, and then call my parents and I'd get in trouble. I looked up at him, and I must've looked scared a little bit because he smiled at me and was like, "I think I'm gonna go surfing. What do you think? Is it too cold out there?" I think I mumbled, "I don't know." I didn't know what to say to him because I didn't really know what surfing was. I mean, I'd seen it on cartoons and TV, but I didn't know anybody surfed in Seawell. I thought he was teasing me or something.

What did you say? Did you tell him the water was cold?
No, umm. It was kinda stupid. I was just a kid, you know. I wasn't supposed to talk to strangers and all that stuff. I think I asked him what surfing was.

I remember his laugh; it was, like, a real laugh. You know? It was like he'd never heard that question before or something. Like…it made no sense to him. I was just a little kid, but I knew he wasn't laughing at me. I could just kinda tell. I remember looking up at him and he was smiling. That was when I noticed he was in his wetsuit, wearing boots and gloves too, but no hood. I just sort of pointed up and down at him and said, "What's that?"

He told me it was a wetsuit and that it kept him warm in the water when he surfed. I remember telling him that was good, because the water was freezin'. That was how our conversation started.

And then he had this beautiful bluish-green surfboard laying up in the soft sand. I just looked up at it at the top of the hill and asked him what it was. I was like, "What's that?" He musta thought I was stupid or something, but he didn't act like it.

He told me that it was a surfboard, a longboard. He told me it was made by a man called, "Dale Velzy." And we walked up there to look at it. I remember that he let me stand on it, on the sand. He dug a hole for the fin, and then lifted me onto it with my bare feet. He told me to bend my knees, and put my arms out and pretend I was riding on a wave in the ocean. I didn't really know what he meant, but I tried to do it like he showed me. And the whole time, he talked to me like I was an adult. You know what I mean? He wasn't treating me like a little baby, even though I was one. He was laughing and it was like he was happy to show someone what he was doing on the beach that day by himself.

Did you see him surf that day?
Yeah, umm, I think I remember what he said to me before he paddled out. He was like, "What's your name? Mine's Sweeney. I'm Sweeney." I told him my name and then he goes, "Well, Erin. It's

good to meet you. I'll make you a deal," I was looking at him, and I was kinda scared again because I was thinking that he was going to ask me about my parents and stuff. But he goes, "I'll go out there and I'll show you what surfing is if you promise to sit here in the sand and watch every wave I catch. Then, after I take a few waves, I'll come in and you can tell me if you like surfing or not."

I remember he said something like that, because he wasn't telling me what to do like my parents always did. He was making a deal with me, and so I just smiled and nodded up at him and then sat down in the warm sand. That was the first day where I realized how much I loved the sand and the beach and stuff. I didn't have anything to do but watch Sweeney surf and look at the sun on the water and play in the sand.

I remember Sweeney picked up his longboard and he made a face, or stuck his tongue out at me, or something, and then ran down the hill to the water and out into the waves. I clapped and got all excited like a little kid, you know? There was still nobody on the beach, so I kinda felt like it was a show just for me. Like some sort of play or something, but then he started surfing and it looked like he was dancing on the water. It wasn't like a play at all, it was like, umm, it was like he was dancing with the waves.

Margaret tells me you're a pretty good surfer yourself. How long have you been surfing?
Well, pretty much since that day when I saw Sweeney surf. My parents made me take some dance classes back then. I went to this studio in downtown Seawell, but I didn't like it much. Everyone said I was pretty good, but I hated dancing in front of people. I liked dancing, that was the fun part, but dancing on a stage with an audience and other dancers and stuff sucked. I remember looking at Sweeney that day, the way he turned the board, and cross-stepped up to the nose and cross-stepped back to the tail and carved—and he made it look so easy. And it's not! At least, it's not easy making it all look as sorta casual as he made it look. He would just glide along the face of the waves and

stall the board and walk out to the nose and then back and then cut back and do drop-knee turns and it seemed like he wasn't moving anything but his legs. His arms and upper body were so, I don't know how to describe it? Umm, he was like, you know when a bull is charging that guy?

The matador?
Yeah, that's it. The matador. Well, Sweeney kind of looked like that. I mean, the waves weren't that big that day, but he still had the kind of style of a matador—really calm and controlled and graceful. That's how they'd describe it at dance lessons, anyway: grace. But the best thing about the whole thing was that he was out there doing it by himself. I mean, he would have been out there all alone if it wasn't for me on the beach. I guess out in California it's really crowded and it's hard to find a place to surf by yourself. And it's kinda like that when I go to Florida with my family for February vacations. You can't really surf alone down there, and it's worse in California. That's what I hear, at least. I mean I haven't been there yet or anything, but that's what my cousins in Dana Point tell me. But out here, in Seawell, I grew up surfing by myself whenever I wanted.

It's the best thing about surfing, I think. You just go out into the ocean with a board and do whatever you want. It gets crowded up at the point breaks in North Seawell, but Seawell Beach is usually empty. Sometimes these seals come by and watch me surf in the fall. They're Northern Fur Seals, I looked it up.

Really? That's cool.
Yeah, I love it. They swim out past where I take off on waves and they crane their necks up out of the water and watch me go down the line on my waves. They're so cute and curious. You can see it in their faces. I like that kind of audience better than the audience at dance shows, but that's just me.

Yeah, I know what you mean. Anything else you want to tell…oh, before I forget, what year was it when you met Sweeney?

Well, I guess I was around eight or nine years old. My birthday's in May and I met him a little before my birthday, so I think that was around 1989. I thought he was wicked old back then, like my parents, because he kinda had a beard and longer hair. But, now, if I had to guess, I suppose he was around twenty.

That sounds about right. I think he was nineteen around then. Anything else?
Umm, I don't think so. I think my lunch break is just about over, and my boss is a real ass...oops! I mean, I gotta get back to work. But one more thing, I saw Sweeney surf one more time, a few years ago. The waves were huge, and he was riding this bright yellow '70s sort of board. It was a single fin and I saw him ride one huge wave. He was definitely like a matador that time. And the more I see people surfing around here the more I realize that no one in Seawell will ever surf like that guy. He had a really nice style. It was like the different boards he used, and the different waves and stuff...he was just in tune with all of it. I'm glad he's the guy who first taught me about surfing.

Oh yeah, umm, before I go: do you know if he's around anymore? Did he really jump off the Pennacook Bridge?

I don't believe he did. So, if you know where he is, maybe you could tell him I've been surfing a long time now thanks to him.

I don't really know where he is. What do you think?
I think he's in Ireland or someplace like that—you know, cold water keeps the crowds away from the good waves. Once you get used to surfing alone, it's hard to go back. At least it is for me. I try to avoid crowds whenever I can. You should look for him in Ireland or South Africa or someplace with cold water. I've been reading about places like that lately.

Well, I guess I gotta go bus some tables. See you later, tell Sweeney I said hi if you see him. I'd like to go surfing with him someday, that'd be the best.
I will, Erin. Take care, and thanks for talking to me.
No problem, see ya later.

UNTITLED

The spread and fold and flex of the frigate birds'
slender, extended tails. Their red chests bulge
above *El Río Chone*, where they soar
and tussle, rise and dive on bent, black wings.

> Specks slipping against the folds
> of low clouds, the birds stitch
> taut patterns along
> the horizon's forested cuff.

The spread and fold and flex of the frigate birds'
swallow-like tails: Their trim, dark silhouettes
above *El Río Chone*, where they soar
and tussle, rise and dive on bent, black wings.

> They narrow in the distance,
> widen to a sliver's width
> through their banked, sharp turns—
> black needles pushed and pulled
> through the overlapped patchwork
> of river, hill and sky.

—Sweeney

(Postmarked in Ecuador, 1994.)

Chapter 2
THE BRAWLING MOUTHS

*I have it from reliable sources that the Trabell brothers, Danny and
Mike, have the filthiest mouths in Seawell. At the time of this interview, both went to Oakland Elementary School, Sweeney's* alma
mater, *in the section of Seawell known as the Oaklands. They look
very much alike in that they are both pale-skinned and fair-haired,
with freckles scattered across the bridges of their noses. The front of
Danny's shirts were perpetually stained with fruit punch or ginger
ale, and Mike never wore a pair of pants that weren't patched or
worn through at the knees. Mike's a year older than Danny, in sixth
and fifth grades respectively, and while they never fight anyone else
they have been suspended three times for beating each other up:
once during a recess game of kickball; once during a school assembly
about personal hygiene; and most recently when they were both
kicked out of their classrooms, found each other in the hallway and
fought about who would be in more trouble when they both got
home.*

*They're tenacious little kids, and I had trouble breaking up
one or two of their fights while I tried to interview them. And, yes,
I now know firsthand that the Trabell brothers have the dirtiest
mouths of any little kids I've ever known. It approaches an art form
with these two.*

*[In the Oakland schoolyard, near the third baseline of the kickball
field]*

So, how did you guys get to know Sweeney?
Mike: We don't know the crazy fuck. We just saw him that day at
the bullring over in Holy Ghost Park.
Danny: Yeah, we snuck in through a hole in the back fence by the
porta-potties. Mike went in one and was like, "Hey, they got a
sink in that one. It was cool." I was like, "You dumbass, that was-
n't a sink! You're supposed to piss in that thing. It's for pissin' in!"
Mike: Danny, shut the hell up. I never said that! *[Turning to me]*
Sorry, he makes stuff up sometimes. Our older cousin told us a
story about a little kid who thought the urinal was a sink, like in a
real bathroom. I wasn't the kid who said it. Danny just likes to
make shit up.
Danny: Fuck you, Mike! I'll say whateverthefuck I want. You're not

my boss just 'cuz you're older than me! Shut up or I'll kick your skinny ass.

Mike: *[Exasperated]* Oh, shut the heck up. Anyways, I was in third grade back then and we just snuck in the back fence. It was just me and Danny, and we climbed up some pallets out back and got on the roof of this barn or something.

Danny: The sign said it was a "Fuckin' Hall." It was funny as shit, I was laughing so hard I almost pissed...mmmph!

Mike: *[Holding his hand over Danny's mouth]* Don't listen to this little shit. It said it was the "Function Hall." He always says that about the sign, he knows what it said. He's stupid.

Danny: *[Escaping Mike's grasp]* If I'm stupid then you're a dumbass, you stupid fuck. *(Danny then jumped up and punched Mike in the temple, Mike screamed and rubbed the side of his head. The boys then began chasing each other around the schoolyard, calling each other every name in the book. I was forced to break Mike's full nelson on Danny over by second base, then Danny bit Mike on his shoulder and they were too pissed off to continue the interview. I brought them to White Hen Pantry, bought them some Slush Puppies and Big League Chew and then we went back to the schoolyard to finish the interview.)*

[Next to the second-base oak tree]

Okay, you were up on the roof and you saw a bullring?

Danny: Yeah, we got up on the roof of the Fuckin' Hall *(shooting a sidelong glance at Mike)* and the Portagees had these weird metal fences set up in the park in a circle. It was some sort of religious party or something for them, so they had this big table with all this food and all the fathers were drunk as shit and there was this crappy music playing on loudspeakers and everyone was too shitfaced to notice us on the roof.

Mike: Not everyone was drunk, like there were mothers and kids there, but they were having this big party. It was cool because we got to see this guy come out dressed in these shiny pants and stupid hat and he fought this fucking huge bull and everyone was cheering and it was pretty cool.

Danny: The bull's horns weren't that pointy, but he was fucking huge. *(The bull's horns were apparently filed down so they would-n't gore the matadors, but the bull still had long enough horns to do some damage.)* I mean I think he weighed, like, ten tons or some-thing.

Mike: Yeah, he was like ten tons and he was all black and sweat-ing and he was so fucking pissed off. He was angrier than my Uncle Ben when he runs out of beer on Saturday. Right Danny?

Danny: Yeah, Uncle Ben comes over and drinks all my Dad's Pabst and then gets fucking pissed and throws the empty cans at the wall and stuff. He swears and throws the cans everywhere. He's a drunk fuck.

Mike: No, I was talking about the bull, you fuckin' loser.

Danny: Oh. Yeah, the bull was madder than Uncle Ben with no beer. You're right.

Mike: So the bull is bleeding a little from running into the metal fence and the guy who was fighting him climbed up the fence and out because he was scared. He was being a pussy.

What about Sweeney? Was he there partying or something—with the Portuguese families? How did he get in the ring?

Danny: *[Excited and shouting]* No, Sweeney wasn't partying with the Portagees, we saw him climb in the same hole in the fence as us! He climbed through and sort of looked up at us, but I don't know if he saw us or not. He just kinda looked up in our direction where we were hiding.

Mike: Yeah, that loony fuck snuck in there just like us, but he walked around to the front of the building. I think he knew some-one there because he was shaking peoples' hands after a while. He started drinking beer and watching the bull running around the ring. It was weird, he was staring at the thing and it was like he didn't even know there was a fucking party going on.

Sweeney snuck in there, and he knew some of the people at the festival?

Danny: We already said that, you dumbass!

Mike: *(Yelling and smacking Danny in the back of the head.)* Hey! Shut the hell up, this guy just bought us Slush Puppies. You better watch your mouth, or I'll kill you.

(At this point, Danny threw his Raspberry Slush Puppy all over Mike and myself and ran away laughing. Mike proceeded to chase him down on the other side of the school, using a nice leg tackle from behind. Danny scraped up his chin and began to cry while Mike flipped him over, pinned down his arms with his knees and gave him a good dose of what they called "The Typewriter Torture." This means that Mike simply poked Danny in the sternum with his index fingers, repeatedly, while yelling "I'm typin', I'm typin'!" until Danny completely spazzed and threw Mike off of him. Finally, Danny chased Mike out into the street and into the woods across from the school on Birch St.)

I called it a day at this point because I was covered in blue Slushy and there was no way I was following those two into that swamp.

[Three days later, at the Trabell household.]

Okay, first tell me why you guys are grounded.

Danny: Me and Mike were fist-fighting in the woods after you left and some guy was driving by and he saw us.

Mike: Yeah, it's all that asshole's fault.

Danny: He said somethin' like, "Hey you two, stop fighting or I'm going to call the police."

Mike: I just gave him the finger and punched Danny in the guts.

Danny: Yeah, he punched me when I wasn't looking. I fell down in the mud. It was gross, it smelled like shit.

Mike: Then the guy got out of his car and he was pointing at us. He was some sort of businessman or geek, he was in a suit, and he said he was gonna call the cops. And I didn't want him to because me and Danny got in trouble last month for doing the can trick to a cop car *[The boys explained that the "can trick" involves stringing fishing line with cans tied to the ends across the street at about car-bumper height so that the driver of the car can't see the fishing line and the whole thing gets wrapped up in the car's bumper.]* How were we supposed to know a cop would drive down the street? It was funny shit!

Danny: Yeah, Mike was saying, "Uh-oh, I smell bacon." And then the stupid cop got the cans all caught up in his axle and wheels and he was clanging down the road. Me and Mike were laughing so hard he heard us, and we couldn't run because we were laughing. That cop was wicked pissed, he grabbed us by our necks and took us home. It killed my neck, but we got a ride in a cop car—which was pretty cool.

Wait a second. Why did you get grounded??

Mike: Oh yeah. So the guy who was going to call the cops on us for fighting in the woods was just being a prick. So I yelled, "Fuck you, you pus-filled shitbag! Get in your car and go fuckyaself!" And then we ran for it. There was no way he could've caught us because we took the shortcut through the swamp and up to Eliot St. We must've laughed at that dumbass for like an hour. Then we went home and Dad was already waiting for us.

Danny: It sucked because I was winning the fight, I was kicking my older brother's ass!

Mike: Yeah, whatever, you dipshit. You weren't even close to winning. You just punched me in the ear once.

Anyways, I guess that guy with the phone went to high school with our Dad, so he recognized us and told my Dad what happened. He told my Dad he was worried because it looked like one of us was bleeding pretty bad. The whole thing is bullshit, and my Dad wasn't even that angry. I think he was kind of laughing about it.

Danny: *[Incredulously]* Yeah, but we still had to stay inside for the whole freakin' weekend and we missed our street hockey game against the Briley School kids. If we lost to those shitheads because of that guy with the phone we're gonna hafta do something about it. I remember what his car looks like. . .

Okay, okay, you guys. Let's get back to the bullfight. You already told me that Sweeney snuck in and was drinking a beer and staring at the bull. What else happened?

Danny: Um...oh yeah, well, what happened next? Mike, what happened...oh yeah! Then, I think another Portagee in a stupid costume climbed into the ring and the bull is bleeding from ramming into the metal fence and stuff. And the bull still looks pretty pissed off and he's doing that thing in the dirt like the bull does in the Droopy Dog cartoon an' everything, and the guy with the cape lets the bull pass him a couple times but the guy looks scared shitless. The Portagee looked like a chickenshit in there. He was holding the cape out and shaking and stuff. It was funny. I wanted to yell stuff at him, but Mike covered my mouth 'cause we woulda gotten thrown outta there.

Mike: Yeah, and then the guy got nailed! You should've seen it! The bull turned around fast and got the guy with one of his horns. The guy went flying! At first I thought it was funny, but then the bull threw the guy off the fence and the whole crowd was quiet and a couple fathers jumped the fence to help the guy on the ground. It was pretty freakin' cool! But the bull was going fuckin' crazy at that point, and he was jumping up and down and kicking and no one could get near the matador guy.

Danny: Then the bull jumped on the guy on the ground. It was gross. We heard the guy's bones break from way on top of the roof.

Mike: It was fucking gross. None of the Portagees could get the bull away from the guy on the ground, an' he was screaming and bleeding and you could see the bone sticking out of his leg. Me and Danny were about to get out of there, because it was scary, but then the bull left the guy alone on the ground and they got him over the fence. And nobody wanted to go in there to try and fight the bull anymore. And that was when Sweeney climbed over the fence. One of his flip flops fell off when he jumped into the ring and so he grabbed it and jumped behind this wooden wall just before the bull almost got him. It was a close one, because that bull was still pissed and he wanted to kill everybody.

Danny: Yeah, someone gave Sweeney a red cape and he was in his flip flops and he didn't have a shirt on and it looked like he was wearing a pair of long shorts—like the guys who surf out at Seawell Beach wear. They were gray ones with a red stripe, I think.

Mike: No, they were blue, shithead. Anyways, all the Portagees started cheering and stuff when Sweeney got in there. He didn't do so good at first. He looked like he was scared, but then he did the thing with the cape like twice and the bull was following it and stuff. So Sweeney started looking like he wasn't that scared at all, and he was smiling and getting the bull to follow the cape over and over.

Danny: Yeah, and all the Portagees started cheering and yelling each time the bull ran by him and missed him. It was pretty fuckin' cool. The bull was getting tired an' shit, an' Sweeney looked like a real bullfighter except he wasn't wearing the shiny costume. He had his hand behind his back and one holding out the cape and he was waving it and stuff like this *[Danny takes off his T-shirt and begins waving it around]*.

Mike: Put your shirt back on, man. You always take your clothes off when you get excited, jeez. Quit bein' a spaz.

So then, after the bull ran by like ten times, it was wicked tired or dizzy or something and Sweeney couldn't get him to chase the cape anymore. It was weird. Then Sweeney. . .

Danny: *[Interrupting his brother]* Oh yeah! I forgot about the coolest part. Then Sweeney starts walking toward the bull like he's dancing or something. It was pretty cool.

Mike: *[Standing up and cross-stepping across the living room to demonstrate]* He was, like, crossing over his steps one after the other and he was getting real close to the bull. The bull was just sorta standing there sweating and breathing heavy and looking at the cape in Sweeney's hand. Then, the best part was when Sweeney kneeled down in front of the bull and stared at his face. It was fucking awesome! It was cooler than that time when Danny broke the back window of the UPS truck with the snowball.

Danny: Yeah, that was pretty funny but this bullfighting thing was way better. The bull was like a foot away from Sweeney and he was genuflexin' like they make us do in church, and they just stared at each other for like a minute or something.

Mike: *[Laughing]* Not "genuflexin'," shithead. "Genuflecting," it means getting down on one knee. But anyway, all the Portagees weren't saying anything; it was wicked quiet. Someone had stopped the music too and Sweeney was just there on one knee like a foot from the bull's face. The bull was breathing heavy and you could see his ribs and he was all bloody with this white stuff coming from his mouth. It was cool.

Danny: *[Standing up to demonstrate]* Yeah, it was the coolest thing I ever seen. Then Sweeney stood up and walked backwards away from the bull, real slow, doing that crossover thing with his feet again. Like this, and he's holding out the cape and stuff. Mike you do it! You do it better than I do.

Mike: *[Mike stands up and backs away from us cross-stepping and pretending he's holding out a cape with one hand behind his back.]* OK, so then the bull chased the cape one more time and missed again! Everyone in the park started yelling and screaming and cheering, and me and Danny were jumping up and down on the roof yelling "*Olé*" and "Sweeney!" and "*Olé*" and all the Portagees were pointing at us and laughing and throwing their hats and beer bottles were smashing everywhere. It was the coolest thing ever.

Danny: Like a week later, I told Dad about it because I thought he would think it was cool. At first he was pissed that we snuck through the fence and climbed on top of a building, but then when I told him what we saw he thought it was the best thing ever. He made me and Mike tell the whole story again to all his friends when they were playing Forty-Fives one night. He let me swear and everything while I was telling it, because Ma wasn't home! All his friends thought it was the best thing they'd ever heard. And me and Mike got to split a glass of beer. It tasted shitty, but I drank it anyway.

Did you guys see what Sweeney did after he climbed out of the ring?

Danny: Yeah, I turned around while everyone was still yelling and screaming and breaking bottles and Sweeney was already out the hole in the fence. So me and Mike climbed down from the roof and tried to catch him.

Mike: I wanted to get his autograph on my shirt or something and tell him how that was the coolest thing ever, but when we climbed through the fence he ran across Clark Rd. and into the woods behind the bus depot. I guess he was headed back to the golf course, 'cause that's where my dad says he lived back then.

Danny: Me and Mike tried to follow him through the depot woods but we couldn't tell where he went. He was fucking fast, he went flyin' through that woods. So we just went home and pretended our backyard was a bullring for like three hours. It was fun.

'Membah that, Mike? When I ran into the bulkhead door and cut my forehead open? Dad was pissed at us for that, huh?

FROM KID TO CONSULTANT

The early days of awe stick in his craw,
but he feels no more than the ghosts of men
in grey suits blown past the downtown bar's door.*
His nimbus was once the whole evening sky,
a wavering miasma of star-flecked green.
He knew, by heart, the liquid accolades
of northern mockingbirds—back when "do-overs"
were law, when mown grass sang within his nostrils.
Before night after night in search of this fade,
he trilled and mucked and trafficked in her words:

> *raw jalopy guy*
> *you are my weary*
> *sparkler sun-bulge*
> *writing letters to the evening*
> *star about our dreaming-*
> *sweetly river*
> *shrouded with jailkid skies.*

Now he feels overfed, insatiate,
in workaday skin. Marlboro smoke wreathes
about his drunk, five-o'clock-shadowed face—
this expert, this consultant, whose days brim
with Muzak and the soft jazz of keyboards.
Who hears the hissed ess-oh-ess of this darkled
grey ghost in his suit? The quiet, mumbled and slurred
ess-oh-ess of this faded requiem shark:

> *pigtails and muzzled*
> *dogs all day long,*
> *heart-patterned pajama*
> *bottoms in coffeeshops*
> *at dawn, pigtails*
> *and muzzled dogs*
> *all day long.*

—Sweeney

*Line adapted from the poem "Aspects of Robinson" by Weldon Kees
(Possibly written during Sweeney's first stay at the Merritt House of
Corrections, 1989-'90. The final draft included the note about the line
adapted from Kees.)

Chapter 3
THE FIFTEENTH–HOLE INCIDENT

I tracked down Gerald Francis, one of the older members at Farannan Golf Course. Gerald was living with his youngest son, Walt, since suffering a mild stroke four months before my visit. Both men had salt and pepper hair, Gerald's was considerably thinner on top than his son's. Both also had unusually large ears, and grey eyes surrounded by especially earnest faces. Gerald's mind was a little scattered at times, but his memory of Sweeney seemed very clear. He was 71 years old when I met with him, and he was unable to speak for any length of time as his voice had somehow been affected in the stroke. Walt did most of the talking for his father. Gerald listened intently in order to make sure his son included all the important details about his old friend, Yardbird Sweeney.

Who taught Sweeney how to golf?
Gerald: *(Nods and points at his own chest, and smiles.)*
Walt: My father taught Sweeney. He told me that none of his own sons had been interested in learning to play golf. And he's right, none of us were interested that much in golf when we were younger. We all played football during high school, and we wrestled in the winter. During the summer we went to different football and wrestling camps, golf seemed like an old man's game to us. We knew Dad was good at golf, one of the best at Farannan, but we figured we had the rest of our lives to learn golf. Anyway, my father told me that he once took Sweeney out on a rainy day when no one was on the course. He took him to the driving range with three or four buckets of balls and taught him how to hit his woods with one bucket, his long to middle irons with another bucket, and then one or two buckets for Sweeney's short game. I think...um, Dad, Sweeney was just a kid then, right?
Gerald: *(Nods and holds up ten fingers, while whispering)* He was only around ten years old! And it only took one day.

One day? You taught him in one day?
Walt: Yeah, my dad always told us about this little kid that hung around on the course all day every summer. He had tried to get Sweeney to play, but Sweeney would only caddy for my father and watch everyone else play. It used to make us laugh how frus-

trated Dad would get about the fact that Sweeney would hang out on that course all day and never hit a single ball. But finally, I think Sweeney must've realized how much Dad wanted to teach him. So they both went out on a misty, foggy day in April. I remember it because it was just after New Englands [the annual high school wrestling tournament] had happened, and I was a senior on the Seawell High team. I'd gotten second at that tournament, I lost to some skinny hick from Timberlane—some high school up in New Hampshire. Dad came home two nights later and was ecstatic that Sweeney had gone golfing with him. It was all he talked about at dinner that night, which was fine with me because I was sick of thinking about coming in second to some backwoods kid.

I'd seen Dad that happy when I'd won the state tournament the year before, so I could see that Sweeney meant a lot to him back then. That night, he told us how he had Sweeney hit four buckets of range balls, and how the kid had a natural swing. Then we heard—and, believe me, we heard this story at the beginning of golf season every year for a long, long time—how Dad and Sweeney went out and played nine holes in the afternoon showers. The course was soaked through from all the April rains, it shouldn't even have been open, probably. But they played and Dad had an awful round, he'd sliced it out of bounds twice, he'd landed in a sand trap that was sitting under three inches of water, he three-putted four greens, and so on and so on. I've practically memorized the whole story.

Dad always ended the story with the same phrase: "Can you believe that a ten-year-old tied me at my own course in the first round of his life? I've been golfing for twenty-some-odd years! For the love of Christ, I can't believe that kid!"

Dad and Sweeney both shot a 45 that day.

I only know a little about golf, is forty-five a good score?
Walt: Forty-five isn't great, but for some kid's first round of golf it was pretty amazing. I mean, even I knew, back on the night Dad told us, that a 45 at Farannan was pretty damn good for a beginner out in the rain and cold. It's like nine over par, I think.
Gerald: *(With a grunt and a pat on Walt's shoulder, Walt and I*

watched as Gerald brought his right hand up under his chin, as if he was going to slap Walt. But then he extended his flat hand away from his body as if he were giving a lost driver directions. Gerald then began whispering a phrase over and over in a hoarse whisper.) Every ball, every ball. He hit it straight, every ball. That kid hit it straight all day long.

Sweeney hit it straight every time?

Walt: *(To his father)* Yeah, Dad, I know. I wasn't going to forget that, don't worry. *(Turning toward me)* Sweeney didn't hit all the balls at the range straight that day, he had some problems with his driver, but Dad always said, and this is a quote, "The damn kid got up to that first tee and hit it straight and just about as long as me. He never looked back. I never saw him duck-hook or slice anything once he got on that course." It really was an amazing story, and I'm not sure if that's really true or not...*(Gerald interrupts by backhanding his son's shoulder—gently, but with a look of consternation on his face)*.

Walt: *(Laughing)* Okay, Okay, Dad insists it's true. I was just kiddin', Dad. Dad swears he didn't embellish the story over the years—but you can take that for what it's worth *(Walt winks at me, and smiles at Gerald who just shakes his head and frowns at his son.)*

Did Sweeney play a lot of golf that summer, or after that? Because I haven't come across many of his friends that remember him as a great golfer.

Walt: Well, Dad says that Sweeney played with him a couple times a week that first summer and fall after he learned, and then they played together regularly during the next several summers. But Sweeney wasn't a member, I mean a junior member, so he had to meet Dad out on number two tee in order to play. Sweeney would play seven holes of golf with Dad, and that would be it. He couldn't play the ninth hole either because the green is right in front of the clubhouse and the members might see him. If Dad was playing with other members, Sweeney wouldn't be waiting at the second tee. He might caddy for Dad if the other guys were around, but he'd never play with a group.

Gerald: *(Gestures insistently with the index finger of his right hand.)*

Walt: *(To his father)* I was getting to that Dad, let me get to it. Jeez. *(Turning to me)* It drives my father crazy that he can't tell you this story. Me and my sisters and brothers always heard these stories when we were younger, but Dad's decided that I tell it the best—besides him, of course *(smiling at Gerald)*. It's driving you crazy isn't it? I know. I'm trying, Dad, I'm trying.

Gerald, what did you mean by shaking your finger?

Gerald: *(Simply points at his son, and then folds his arms and nods while pursing his lips and giving a little shrug.)*

Walt: He meant that Sweeney was known to play alone in the early morning or late evening. Like you always used to say, Dad, "The kid could and would play in the dark." See, one of the things that drove my father nuts about Sweeney is that he was usually alone on the course—other than when he was running around with your father, Owen. My dad loved Farannan because he could go down there and drink beers and bullshit in the morning, go out and play a round with his buddies, then come back to the bar overlooking the ninth hole and sit and drink beers in the shade and bullshit about the round he'd had or talk trash about the other guys on the course that day. My dad loved the social aspects of golf, but Sweeney hated it. I guess Sweeney only ever played with my Dad and by himself.

Yeah, my father Patrick tells me he only hit balls with Sweeney a few times when they were kids, but that the two of them hung out on the course a lot together back then. Although, I heard Sweeney did play in one of the City Tourneys, and didn't he almost win it? I thought you had to be a member to play in it?

Walt: You do. I mean, Sweeney joined up one year because he'd seen that annoying lawyer from Mt. Pheasant Country Club win it. That's how Dad tells it.

Dad, what was that guy's name, that idiot with the white pants and hair plugs? I always forget his name.

Gerald: *(Laughing and whispering)* Harold, Harold Crasspus, that bastard.

Walt: That's right! Harold Crasspus. He thought he was the best golfer Seawell had ever seen. And he'd just flat out tell you that when you talked to him. He was just a bastard, and no one liked him. Even the guys at Mt. Pheasant hated him. Just a rich prick, you know? He was some semi-retired partner in a law firm in Concord, and he had all the time in the world to golf. The guys at Mt. Pheasant told me he was always moaning and complaining about women on the course and how many black guys had joined the club. Just an all-around idiot, you know. So...wait, what was I talking about before Crasspus?

Gerald: *(Rolls his eyes and takes a drink from his tea.)*

Walt: Alright, alright Dad, take it easy, I remember. I was saying how Sweeney had never played golf with other people and he didn't really like the whole country-club atmosphere of the thing. But he was an athlete, and was kinda competitive as I understand. My dad arranged with the guys at Farannan to let Sweeney join as a junior member. Most of the guys knew of Sweeney. For years, Sweeney'd sold them back the balls they lost in the woods and water. Dad said a few of the sour old guys down at Farannan complained about him here and there, but almost everyone liked the kid.

Sweeney was fifteen, or at least that's what he told my father, at the time when they let him join. My father and a couple of the other old guys paid Sweeney's membership dues, which weren't much for a junior member. *(Turning toward his father)* Something like two-hundred bucks, or so. Right, Dad?

Gerald: *(Squints, in an effort to remember and then nods and gives the "somewhere-near-that-amount" wiggle of his left hand.)*

Walt: Yeah, so it was around two-hundred or two-fifty, this is back in '85, I think. Sweeney promised he would beat the Crasspus guy. Sweeney and my father sometimes talked about the bad stuff that's associated with golf whenever they played their seven holes together. Sweeney hated that rich-white-guys-only feel of the game, and my Dad did too. We're part Portuguese, and my Dad has had to ignore more than a few

"Portagee" comments down at Farannan from some of the members he doesn't get along with. Sweeney might have been part Hispanic or something, too. I don't know. My dad said he had dark skin and black hair, but no one really knew. He could've been Black Irish for all we know. Anyway, Sweeney had heard Crasspus making comments during previous City Tourneys about how Farannan had the most "niggers" of any of the clubs, and how it was a trashy course, and stuff like that. And that was why he agreed to play in the Cities and try to beat Crasspus.

Didn't Sweeney pull some pranks on Harold Crasspus during one of the previous Cities?

Gerald: *(Laughs, smiles, and gestures at Walt with a sweep of his right hand as if to say, "Go ahead, tell him, you know the story." He then sat back in his chair with his arms folded, a broad smile on his face.)*

Walt: Oh yeah, there were two big pranks that Sweeney pulled off. But two years before he had decided to even play in the Tourney, he pulled off the first good one. What Sweeney did was, he figured out what ball Crasspus was playing. The year before, he heard Crasspus spouting about how he only played Titleist Balatas, every ball a number four. I guess Sweeney combed the woods and ponds that whole next year to find all the Titleist Fours that he could. He must've had two hund...

Gerald: *(Leans forward and delivers a slap to his son's shoulder, and wags his finger at him and begins whispering hoarsely)* You can't tell it like that, you're telling the story wrong. Set it up, Walt. For the love of Christ, set it up and tell the story right. Tell it like I told you and your mother when it happened!

Walt: Okay, Dad, I'm sorry. Relax, jeez, you'll wear yourself out. I'll tell it right. Sit back, I promise *(gently eases his father back into his chair)*. I'm sorry. You're right. I'll start over. You just gotta promise to relax, or I'll have to tell Owen this stuff without you here as creative director. You can't handle too much stress, okay? *(Turning toward me)* Jeez, that's the most he's even tried to say for months. He's right though, I did screw up there. Let me start again.

So Crasspus is leading the Cities for the fourth year in a row. As much as he was a prick, he was a really good golfer. It was his life. Sweeney knew this, and Sweeney's life was connected to golf in a different sort of way. My Dad said that Sweeney just played golf because it was a game. Granted, it was a game that "requires exceptional mental and physical dexterity," as Dad always said. But Dad told us that Sweeney was a natural, so he just played because it was challenging and simple at the same time. It had the potential to be beautiful—in a way—you know, just using the right club to hit the right shot at the right time. *(Walt looks over at Gerald to see if he is telling the story properly. Gerald gives a single thumbs-up from the crook of his folded arms, coupled with a wink.)* Well, I guess I'm on the right track here, so I'll keep going.

Sweeney hated Crasspus and Crasspus just didn't pay much attention to anything he might have heard about Sweeney. But after the infamous "Fifteenth-Hole Incident" he probably began believing in Sweeney a little more. See, what Sweeney did was wait by the sixth hole, in the woods, during the last round of the City Tourney. There's no fifteenth hole at Farannan, because it's a nine-hole course, so everyone plays each hole twice from different tee positions for the second round. Crasspus was playing against some slouch from Zephyr Country Club. They were the two leaders of the Tourney that year, so they were the last group on the course. Crasspus had a three-shot lead, going into the fifteenth hole and it didn't look good for that guy from Zephyr. So they tee up on the fifteenth, and it's like a short, par-four hole. Some guys can hit the green from the tee. It would make sense not to go for the green if you were Crasspus, since he had the lead. I mean, most guys would play it safe and lay-up and then hit a pitching wedge from like fifty yards out. But Sweeney knew Crasspus was an arrogant bastard, and that he'd go for the green anyways. At least, that's what Sweeney was hoping for.

Of course, Sweeney was right. Crasspus took out his driver or three wood and went for the green. He just cleared the front sand trap and his ball ended up on the green. From the tee, you could see that it rolled to the back, around fifteen or twenty feet from the hole. The guy from Zephyr had no choice but to try the same thing, he had to try and catch Crasspus. The Zephyr guy ends up hitting the back of the green, but the ball didn't stick—it rolled off the back fringe and down the hill near the woods.

Here's what is pretty amazing about this prank: Sweeney had figured out that as the gallery and the two golfers walked down from the tee into the gully in the fairway, none of them would be able to see the surface of the green. The green was a little elevated, but the big sand trap in front had a, um…a sort of steep wall of sand that blocked the view of the green. Sweeney had very little time to pull off the prank, but he did it.

What he did was he took about a hundred and fifty or two hundred Titleist Fours and scattered them all over the green—all around Crasspus's ball on the back of the green. None of the Titleists were on the fringe or in the rough, they were all on the green. When Crasspus got up to the green, swaggering and carrying on about reaching the green with one shot, his jaw dropped. My Dad was there in the gallery, hoping that Crasspus would choke and lose it on the last four holes.

Gerald: *(Leans forward with his elbows on his knees, his head in his hands. He is laughing silently, with the occasional wheeze, he is laughing hysterically.)*

Walt: *(Gesturing at his father, and laughing himself.)* Oh, this story…this story doesn't get old for the old man. And, hold on, I'm sorry *(Trying to contain his laughter)*. I'm sorry, okay….Wooo, I guess it doesn't really get old for me either (Laughs).

Okay, I'll keep going. Dad, rein it in, you're losing it *(More laughter from both)*!

Alright, I've seen Crasspus and I know he's got these god-awful hair plugs. He was one of the first guys, back in the '80s, to get hair plugs. My dad swears that when Crasspus saw the two hundred balls on the green—see, Sweeney had snuck up and dumped what must've been a trash-barrel full of golf balls onto the green—my dad swears that Crasspus lost it so bad that he pulled out his own hair plugs. Ha! How 'bout that shit? The whole gallery was dyin' laughing, and no one knew what the hell to do or how the hell all the balls had gotten there. There was just an empty trash barrel and no sign of Sweeney anywhere.

It was a small gallery of about fifty people—mostly from Zephyr, watching their guy—because nobody else wanted to see Crasspus win again. Everyone was pretty buzzed, because they sell beers on the course and it's usually a pretty good all-day party. So there's like fifty people laughing uncontrollably at Crasspus, and he's there pulling his hair plugs out and just freaking and yelling and swearing. It made no sense to anyone, how it happened, but it was perfect. It livened up that party.

Somebody, I think it was Sully, ran back to the clubhouse bar to tell everyone what had happened. I'd snuck in the bar and was getting a little bombed in the side room when Sully ran in and yelled, "You guys! You guys! Come check this out. Someone just fucked Crasspus. Somebody dropped like a thousand Titleist Fours on the fifteenth green. We can't find his damn ball!" At that point, like two hundred people ran down the eighth and ninth fairways with their beers in their hands and then over to the "Fifteenth-Hole Incident," which is what people began calling it that day.

Gerald: (*Is sitting back with folded arms, smiling broadly, occasionally wiping the tears from the corners of his eyes. He then takes out a hanky, unfolds it carefully and blows his nose with a loud honking noise over and over.*)

Walt: Whoa! Easy, Dad, you'll blow a gasket there. God, we love this story, don't we? And, Owen, you know how serious people in Seawell are about the City Tournament. I mean, it's a pretty big party but the golfers in Seawell act like it's a sacred event, like a major tournament or something. So many people across the city were pissed about the prank, but so many non-golfers loved that it happened. The next few years of the Tourney were huge—just huge drunkfests with golf getting played somewhere nearby. It was great. I wish it was still like that.

So who won the Cities that year? How did Harold Crasspus finish that hole?

Walt: Well, actually, yeah, Dad weren't you an official that year? Yeah, he was, because he had won the thing many years before that—when I was just a little kid. I remember I was glad he was an official because that kept him from catching me sneaking beers in the bar.

So I get to the green, and Crasspus is just pissed off beyond belief. He's fuming. And my dad and the other officials from the other clubs rule that the entire hole has to be replayed by both golfers. I heard my dad pushing for the ruling that the Zephyr guy could play out his ball since his wasn't on the green, and Crasspus would have to replay the hole—but that didn't go over too well. Made sense to me. I mean, why penalize the Zephyr guy? He didn't do anything, and we could see his ball sitting in the short rough behind the green.

To make a long story short, Crasspus and the Zephyr guy replayed it and both guys hit the green from the tee. But, once they got down to the green to putt it seemed like Crasspus was spooked or something. He kept squinting into the woods and up into the trees as he approached the green.

The gallery was now about three hundred people, and a bunch of us were pretty drunk and rowdy. We were heckling Crasspus, and yelling stuff about "The Farannan Yeti."

I'll never forget the sight of Crasspus bent over his ten-foot putt for par when they replayed the hole. He looked like some sort of falcon or hawk had tried to carry him off by the hair. He was pretty shaky. It was hilarious. We were all quiet when he stroked the putt and left it about four feet short of the hole. Everyone in the gallery, even some guys from Mt. Pheasant, let up a huge cheer. The Zephyr guy had birdied the hole and was now only one shot back from Crasspus. Crasspus had four-putted! Four-putted! The guy was a mess.

Did the Zephyr guy end up beating Crasspus? They had three holes left, right? Who won?
Gerald: (*In a hoarse whisper.*) The Zephyr guy won it on the first playoff hole. Crasspus fell apart. It's how he got the nickname. Harold "House-ah-Cards" Crasspus.

OUT-OF-BOUNDS

Before I went to prison, years ago,
I built a simple footbridge in the woods
north of hole number six. There was a stand
of honey ash tucked behind the swamp,
about two-hundred yards from the fairway,
beyond "The Pit" where the high school kids drank.
I lived beneath those ash, for several years.
Spring, fall, winter and summer in an old
trawler, long since retired, perched on oil drums
and stacks of beam ends. A rank, weedy creek—
more like a wet ditch—squabbled and meandered
around my boat, my refuge run aground.
My friends would visit and we'd drink some beers,
insult each other, then strive to one-up
the other guy with old stories of getting
drunk—until they'd leave and inevitably
trip into the muskbush by the muddy creek.
So I decided to build them a bridge,
something to catch their drunk stumbles and stop
their harsh, predictable bitching and moaning.

This was all just before I went away,
well after I began to write my poems,
but well before my friends abandoned me.
My blue-collar friends shied from me and my
poems as most forgot about those things
that we dreamt, dwelled and thrived on as little kids.
Some shied from things that didn't reek of work,
or rhyme like sports, sing like assembly lines.
The ring of earnings, the shine of long weekends,
these were the new rhythms of their lifetimes.
I don't blame anyone, but when I laid
my simple bridge over that no-name ditch—
as I leapt into what I loved—they left.

I wanted to write, I knew nothing else.
I avoided the dull thud of the clock-punch,
rode a bike, lived in an old wooden boat,
and wrote my poems from my grove of trees.

I soon became "What-a-Waste," "Lazy-Bastard"
and "That-Loony-Fuck."
                                  I'm Sweeney Out-of-Bounds
and my bridge rots and sinks into the oily
pockets of mud—black bed of the bull frog.

I have known friends, I have known the small comforts
of visits—shared starlight seen through the shifting
canopy of ash. I have notched a dying
alder's thick trunk, chopped on the southern side
to fell the tree to the north. I have known the heft
of the plane in my palm, the shaving down of raw
materials. I've slowly sculpted, reaped,
parsed, pieced, composed, chipped at and drawn
a bridge to my world.
                                  And now I know the cold
of the winter roost, the ice-encrusted nest
leaning and creaking high above the blue,
dead snow of a February out of bounds.

—Sweeney

(Written in longhand on the back of a rifle-range target, postmarked in
Minnesota, 1995. For more on Sweeney's boat see Appendix B, *The
Kemp Aaberg.*)

Chapter 4

Ghost-Riding Robin Hood

The following is an interview with Yardbird Sweeney's landscaping boss Miguel Obregon. Everyone calls Miguel "Micky" or "Goatboy" in Seawell. He and Sweeney went to high school together, played baseball together and started mowing lawns together in the summers. Micky weighs in at about 180, with a small beer belly and a tuft of black beard on his chin. He has olive skin, black hair and blue eyes. His parents are originally from Puerto Rico. Sweeney and Micky had more than forty lawns all over Seawell when they were just seniors in high school. After graduation they expanded into tree maintenance and removal. Soon after graduation, Sweeney gave his share of the business to Micky. Periodically, Sweeney returned to Seawell and worked as Micky's foreman for the tree crew.

When I finally got a chance to speak with Micky—in May, approximately twelve years after he and Sweeney had mown their first lawns together—he'd sold the lawn maintenance side of the business. Micky is now the Head Groundskeeper at Farannan Golf Course, and he is also owner/operator of the Flintmere Treescaping business. Flintmere has captured the bid for the City of Seawell's tree work for the past five years.

During this interview, at times, Micky seemed reluctant to talk. I tried to draw information out of him without antagonizing him. By the latter stages of our talk, Micky was on a roll so I got out of his way and stopped asking questions.

Micky, it's nice to finally get to talk to you. You're a busy guy.
Yeah, sorry. You shoulda tried me back in December. We didn't have any work back then. I sat around twiddlin' my damn thumbs for weeks. Didn't know what to do with myself.

Anyways, whaddaya wanna talk about? If you're looking for Sweeney, and you think I know where the silly bastard is, you're wrong. I don't know shit. I haven't talked to the guy in a coupla years. He was s'posed to show last June for tree work, but he never did. He told me he'd be back for a big job we had coming up. He said that before he left that winter, or, wait, I guess that was two years ago now. Anyways, he usually told me the truth about that stuff. Always did, until that year. But...he was a no-show. Wait a sec, *d'you* know where that prick is?

No, I was kind of hoping you did. People were telling me you proba-
bly know, but that's okay. Nobody seems to know. Did he say where
he was going when he left, what was it, over two years ago?
Yeah, it was October a couple years ago. And, no, he didn't say
where he was going. He never, ever, tole me where the fuck he
was going. Never. He only useta tell me when he was coming
back. I mean, he always just went somewhere to surf, I think. And
then he'd come back to Seawell around the time he tole me he
would, give or take a couple months.

        I'd be sitting in McSwiggans, or The Temple Bar and he'd
come up to me outta nowhere. It always freaked me out. I'd be
half in the bag talkin' to some woman or something and then he'd
suddenly be sitting across the bar from me. One time, when we
were both around twenty—we're the same age, ya know—he
actually managed to sit down next to me at the muthafuckin' bar
without me seein' him. I look to my left and he looks me in the
face and says, "Hey, Micky. How's things? Can you get an old
friend that's down on his luck a beer or two?"

        I still have no idea how he got on my left, in the chair
next to me in The Temple. You been there?

Is it called the Skeff now?
Yeah, some new guys bought it. Same place.

Yeah, I've been there. It's a tiny place.
Yeah, it's just a tiny dive, ya know. But somehow, that bastard
was sitting next to me. I hadn't see him in like a year. "Hey,
Micky. How's things? Can you get an old friend that's down..." Can
you believe he says that type of shit?

So, what's your opinion on the police finding Sweeney's bike
beneath the Pennacook Bridge a week after he'd disappeared?
You know, no one's ever asked me whether I thought Sweeney
jumped or took off to Mexico or somewheres. It's weird, it's like
everyone thinks I'm gonna get pissed off or cry in my beer or
something if they asked me. Everyone still talks about it now and
then. Some drunk fuck will say he saw Sweeney down on Middle

St., goin' into Stella's or some stupid shit like that, and then everyone will freak out and talk about Sweeney-this and Sweeney-that. I hear it in the bars now and then, some of the guys have running bets that he didn't jump and that he'll be back on such-an'-such a date. I betcha about a thousand cases of beer will change hands the day Sweeney runs outta money and comes back to Seawell to work for me.

So you don't think he jumped from the bridge?
It's all a load of bullshit, if you ask me. I mean, the fuckin' guy coulda jumped, he coulda gone to fuckin' Botswana to learn how to hunt rabid wombats for all we know! What's the difference? We'll never know, unless he shows up back in Seawell one night down at The Wardin.

You don't care?
I don't know, kid. They didn't look too hard for a body, and the bike was locked. I'd love to say that the bike was locked so that means someone else put the bike out there and Sweeney'll be back. But I don't know. The stupid prick never locked his bike before that, half the time he'd just ghost-ride the damn thing toward the sidewalk in front of whatever bar he was gracing with his presence. But he could be fuckin' with my head, too. He'd do that kind of shit. So where the hell does that leave us?

I'm not sure I follow?
I mean, the guy rode around town on that old three-speed bike. It was a chocolate-brown piece of work. It was called "The Robin Hood." You could barely see the scratched-up name painted on the side. Sweeney would just ride it out from the golf course to whatever bar we were all going to and just slip off the back of the bike and let it park itself. I useta just drive around and look for that bike stuck in a snowbank somewhere in North Seawell and then I'd know what bar he was in. He didn't give a shit about the bike so he never bothered with chains and a lock.

Is ghost-riding when you just push the bike with no one on it?

Yeah, we all did it when we were kids, ya know? The Robin Hood could be ghost-ridden with pretty good accuracy. I don't think that piece of shit ever sat in a bike rack in its life, and it sure as hell was never locked up until the day the cops found it near the Pennacook.

Do you think Sweeney locked it up just to be funny or did someone else put the bike out there as a sort of joke after Sweeney disappeared?
Well, that's a good theory, that one about someone else putting the bike out there. It's somethin' I thought about a little bit, but it's dogshit! Because the bike was always in my garage out on the golf course—where Sweeney kept it. And everyone thinks Sweeney took off a week before the bike was found, but that's not how I see it.

The bike was in your garage during the week that Sweeney had supposedly taken off?
Yeah, the bike was there on Tuesday when I went in to get some tools. I think I was looking for some rakes or somethin', and the bike was there. I remember it was there because Sweeney had stopped working for me the Friday before and the bike was gone for the weekend. Everyone said on Sunday that Sweeney was gone again, but the bike was back on Tuesday. So I don't know where he was in Seawell but he didn't leave when everyone thought he did.

When did they find it by the Pennacook?
I think I read in the papers that they found it on a Friday morning, at like three in the morning or something. Most of the cops in Seawell know Sweeney's bike by sight.

Was the bike in your garage until Thursday night or Friday morning?
I didn't go in the garage much that week because we were just about done with work back then. It was a bad October that year, so most of the leaves were down by mid-October and me and

Sweeney and the other guys had done our fall cleanups by the second week of November. We did like three straight weeks of fall cleanups. Just about raked my fuckin' arms off that year, and then Sweeney said he was taking off when we were done. Some of the guys on the crew spread the word in the bars that he was leaving when work was done, and it went from there. But, like I said, the bike was there that Tuesday and then I saw it on Thursday night at about seven. I was on my way down to The Wardin for the beer-boiled hot dogs and football, and I was putting the rakes back in the garage. The bike was there, and one of my chains and padlocks was hangin' from the handlebars. I remember stopping for a sec, because the chain-and-lock thing made me think.

So the chain and padlock that were on the bike under the bridge came from your garage, and Sweeney had a key to your garage?
Yeah, we used to use the chains on the trailer to lock down the blowers and the Walker mower while we were driving from job to job. But, like I said, Sweeney never locked the damn bike up so I thought he was going to use the chain and lock for something else that Thursday night when I saw it. Didn't matter to me, because we were done with for the season pretty much.

And he had a key to your garage?
Yeah, me and him had the only keys. I think. Maybe Will has one now, but not back then. So, yeah, just me and Sweeney at that time.

Would this mean that Sweeney took the bike and lock out of the garage and rode it over to the bridge?
I don't know, man. Do I look like Agatha-fuckin'-Christie? I have no idea if Sweeney did it, really. Someone could've stolen or found his key or something. Who knows?

I have to be honest with you Mick, you're not clearing much up for me.
Yeah, no shit. Welcome to the club. Anybody who knew the guy was only worse off for it in the head *(Laughs)*.

What do you mean by that? From what I hear, you and Sweeney were just about best friends.
Yeah, yeah, I'm just kiddin'. Me, him and your dad were all pretty tight. But the guy did mess with your head if you knew him. It was just how he was. He didn't always do it on purpose either. I mean, he was so much on his own level that you couldn't figure him out for the life of ya.

Was he as smart as some other people have told me?
Oh, the fuckin' guy was brilliant. He shoulduv gone to some Ivy League school or something, but he knew what he wanted to do and did it. That was the thing, if I can tell you anything that I figured out about the guy—and it ain't much—Sweeney made a decision early on to do what he wanted to do. Once his parents cut out, he did whatever he wanted whenever he felt like it.

Everyone has been telling me stories about Sweeney, and how they came to know him. You must have a few good ones.
Oh, I got shit I can't even tell you about. I got stories from when we were fourteen, drinkin' beers and getting' in trouble—shit that's pretty damn funny.

You want to share any with me?
Share? What the fuck is this, "Romper Room" or something?

Um…I thought that you would want…
I'm just fuckin' with ya. I'll tell you a story, but you only get one. 'Cuz, yeah, the guy is my friend, but I'm not doing any of that "Sweeney-this and Sweeney-that" bullshit that all these other guys do. That shit sucks, and Sweeney would be the first to tell you that if he was here. But, like I said, I got a story that'll give you all you need to know about the guy.

Good, good, for a minute there I thought you were getting pissed off with me.
Nah, I'm always kind of angry, but that's because I'm a prick. Don't worry about it. I'll tell you a story, but none of that high-

school shit. Sweeney was a high-school hero, but he let that all go. He never talked about how he called a one-hitter against Galloway with that ham-an'-egger, Miren, on the mound. That was impressive shit, but he never said shit about it or anything about the stupid stuff we did back then to get in trouble when we were teenagers. He let it all go, and so I'll follow his lead on that.

I'll tell you about the day he got outta Merritt [House of Corrections]. He was in there for around eighteen months or something.

I was at the garage at Farannan, trying to change out the blades on the mowers one last time for the year. I had my wrench in one hand, and one of the thirty-six inch mowers up. The fucking blades weren't coming off, so I was getting pissed. It was early, around seven or so, and I had six or eight lawns to get to that day.

So this was while you were working at the golf course, but before you sold off the lawn maintenance section of the business?
Yeah, I dabbled in both for a while before I decided to work at the course and keep the tree work. Once I got the contract to do the city's tree work, I gave up all that lawn shit and sold all the mowers.

But, yeah, I was in the garage trying to pull off the blades and in walks Sweeney. It was a shitty, cloudy day. I was hoping the rain and sleet would hold off so I could do these lawns for the last time that year. So, he walks in and I says to him, like I was angry or something, "Oh, look who it is. You're a little early. Is that rain holding off?" He just laughed a little and said, "You mean snow? It hasn't started yet. And, by the way, you owe me twenty-five bucks for the cab, asshole."

I was supposed to pick him up at noon at Merritt. But he told me he'd gotten out early. He'd talked Leo Luque into letting him out a few hours early. So I says, "You talked a fucking prison guard into letting you out early because you thought the waves were good? How the hell…"

He says, "Well, I didn't tell him it was 'cuz of the waves. But he kinda owed me one from some other stuff I did for him.

What's six hours or so after eighteen months, ya know?"

By then, I was up off the floor and we shook hands and I told him it was good that he was out and stuff like that. I told him that I had started surfing a little before he went into Merritt, and that someone had to use all of his boards up in the rafters of the garage while he was gone. He says to me, "You? Surf? Goatboy, what the hell is that about? You could barely swim last time I saw you." He'd been calling me "Goatboy" since I'd grown my first scruff on my chin when I was like sixteen. The name stuck for a while, but had sort of faded since he was gone. I wasn't too happy to hear it again, so I told him to go fuck himself about the nickname, and we laughed. Even though I was kinda serious.

But then *he* got a little serious and started to ask me about his favorite surfboard, his baby. Before he could even get upset I told him I hadn't touched the damn thing. I knew that board was sacred to him for some reason, and I knew not to use it while he wasn't around. He loved that board—more than The Robin Hood, even. He calmed down pretty quick when he saw the board off by itself in the rafters. He said that that board was the one he'd been thinking about all that time in Merritt. It was this beautiful yellow, single fin, seventies-style board he got during one of his trips. He never told me where exactly he got it.

But, next thing I know, he's got his winter wetsuit out and is looking for his boots and gloves. I'd put all the stuff in a locker for him and I got it out and handed it over. I was like, "Sweeney you better have done about a million pushups and sit-ups back in Merritt 'cuz it's fuckin' big out there today."

He just kind of quieted down at that point, mumbled "I know, I know," and started putting on his wetsuit. I was trying to get him to skip the morning session and to wait for the tide to go back out in the afternoon. I told him I would take him up to the points later on, up in North Seawell. I was just trying to get him to stay away from the beachbreak down on Seawell Beach. I'd checked it when I came into work, like I did every day since I'd started surfing, and it was double- to triple-overhead out there. It was out of control. Way too big for me to even think about surfing. I wasn't even going in up at the points, where it was a little more in-control, but I just told Sweeney that to try and get him to wait until later to surf. I was thinking that maybe someone else would be out somewhere and we could keep an eye on Sweeney since he hadn't surfed in so long. I mean, I'd be watching from the beach wherever we went, but some of the other locals would be psyched to surf with Sweeney again. They'd know to just keep an eye out for him since he'd just gotten out an' stuff.

But, after the first few minutes of trying to get Sweeney to wait, I could tell that there was no chance in that happening. He was quiet and focused. He was in his suit, and was just about to pull the hood over his head, but he realized he had the wrong boots. He had his summertime, thin boots. He needed his five-millimeter boots because it was late-October, and the water was pretty cold by then.

I told him to wax up the Hot Buttered—yeah, that's what it was, it was a Hot Buttered board from Australia. I told him to wax up and I looked for some five-mil boots for him. I couldn't find mine or his at that point, and Sweeney just wasn't gonna wait. I knew that much. He had waxed the board, pulled on his hood, and had his lobster-claw mittens on already. I looked up at him and he says, "Fuck it, Goatboy, I don't need boots today." And he walked out the door.

I was like, "Wait, man, you gotta at least wear the three-mils!" He was gone. I run outside, and he's already trotting out of the woods toward the sixth and seventh holes.

I had to see this shit.

I grabbed my phone and called up a couple of the locals from North Seawell and Sun Valley and told them what was going on. I only got through to one of the guys, Mike O'Dowd, and he said he'd be down as fast as he could.

I jumped on the Walker mower, the ride-on mower, and headed toward the seventh fairway. I was goin' as fast as I could, and those things move pretty good, so I was catchin' up to Sweeney. But it'd started flurrying these big fat white flakes. It was coming down pretty hard, actually. It was more than a flurry, kind of a snow squall—which is a little weird for October, but, then again, it's New England so it's not that weird.

It was hard to see Sweeney, he was just turning up along the edge of the woods on the right side of number seven. I could see him in his all-black wetsuit jogging through the snow, with that beautiful yellow board under his left arm. But it was coming down really hard right then. The flakes were huge and wet, and falling straight down, and sticking to everything. There wasn't much wind, so I guess it wasn't a squall, really, but it was just like a curtain of fat white flakes falling. There was already a white coat of snow over most of the grass on the course. As I cut across the sixth hole I could see that Sweeney had jogged along the tree line around the green and up the seventh. His bare feet were leaving a dark trail of footprints through the grass and fallen leaves.

I finally caught up with him about a hundred yards off the seventh tee. I pulled up alongside and says to him, "Are your damn feet feelin' like bricks by now? Take these fuckin' boots, man. At least wear something." I tried to hand him the three-mils.

He looked over at me for a split second, and I just stopped talking and kept driving along next to him. His eyes were this piercing green...just intense. He was going in without the boots and, since I knew the guy pretty well, I could tell he had no time for my bullshit. He had that look that says he only has time for the essential shit. Sometimes he used to look like that right before a fight started, or before we had a sketchy tree job to do. I used to see him look like that after he'd had a few beers—and those nights always turned into all-nighters, somehow.

So I just gave it up, I was like, "Okay, okay, calm-the-fuck-down! But don't expect me to swim out there and save your jailbird ass. You're on your own." And then I asked him, "Have you even checked it, yet?"

He says, without even looking at me, "Yeah, it's the biggest it's been in my life. It's from those three huge storms off the coast. I know what's up."

I go, "Alright, alright. Just checking. Water's about 46 or 47 degrees, I'd say. It was choppy this morning, but the wind seems to be dying or something. The tide was all the way out about two hours ago, so now it should be pushing over the mid-tide sandbars, with the storm surge, on the inside. The outside sets will be feathering way out there. It should be about as good as it's gonna get today."

"No shit?" he says, with a sort of sarcastic grin. He knew the conditions, no doubt about it. And by this time the snow was letting up a little. I mean, the flakes were a little smaller, anyway.

"Yeah, so, the sets are coming pretty close together. Probably only ten minutes or less between the pulses. These are the biggest storms we've seen in a few years, and they're pushing some ten- to fifteen-foot waves in here. It's probably gonna get bigger while you're out there, too."

"Goatboy, Jesus, I didn't know you *really* started surfing." he says.

"Yeah, I'm on it. I check this place every day. I been keeping an eye on it for you while you were gone. A seal couldn't beach its fat ass around here without me seein' it."

I remember I couldn't help smiling at the guy. I was just chuggin' along on the mower, smilin'. It was really good to see him, ya know? I'd been waiting to go for a surf with Sweeney for a long time, since he went into Merritt, but this time I was only gonna get to watch. It didn't matter to me, I didn't give a fuck— as long as Sweeney was out I felt pretty good.

You'd fuckin' think *I'd* been in jail or something, huh? It was just that he was an old friend, and it seemed like he was back on track, he was back in Seawell, it all felt pretty good to me. I don't know if Sweeney felt that way or not.

By this point, we were down on the right side of the green. We'd covered five-hundred-and-fifty-some-odd yards pretty quickly. The snow was letting up to a light flurry. Sweeney stopped before he climbed down the rocks behind the green. I turned off the mower.

"Anything else I should know?" he says to me, while he was staring out at the ocean.

And he was humoring me, believe me. This guy knew more about that surf spot than anyone. He'd been surfing there as long as I'd known him, and I think he started like five or six years before I met him. But I tole him what I thought anyway, I guess I kinda wanted to show him that I was into it, you know? So I says, "It should be linin' up outside The Little Rocks and walling up all the way to Triangles. If you get the right wave, something more from the east than the north, you might get a reform all the way through to the inside."

"Thanks, Goatboy. that's good stuff. How 'bout a beer later? I want to go down to The Skeff and then over to McSwiggans." I remember he wanted to see Skidsy bartending over at McSwiggans.

I was like, "Yup. Skidsy's still there. He'll never leave that fuckin' place. You know that."

Then he sort of jumped down onto the beach and stood in the soft sand for a few minutes. I was yelling at him to hurry his ass up, that I was cold as hell and stuff like that, just givin' him shit. He pretty much ignored me.

As he paddles out, there was this long lull. He only had to push under two or three waves on his way out. The ocean went nearly flat, I swear to God. It was eerie. I mean, I'm sitting there on my riding mower, cold as hell, it's still snowing a little bit, and out he goes into the biggest fuckin' day Seawell has seen in like thirty years—and the Atlantic goes almost flat for his paddle out.

He gets outside and sits up on the board. It was right around then I realized he didn't put on a leash. The board didn't even have a leash plug. I was fuckin' nervous, there was a lot of water moving around out there. A set was coming in, it looked like it was going to close out across all of Seawell Beach, and he's sitting out there on a board he hasn't ridden in two years. There was no doubt in my mind that I was going to have to swim out there and save him. As the set lined up on the horizon, I just started screaming and whistling as loud as I could. I stood up on the seat of the mower, the thing's springs were squealing, and I'm yelling at the silly bastard at the top of my lungs. I know he didn't hear me, but he starts scratching for the horizon to get over the set. He gets through it okay, and I'm relieved so I kinda crouch down on the mower, just shaking my head and hoping that Mike O'Dowd comes down from up north in case Sweeney needs help.

I couldn't see anyone on the entire beach, it was deserted.

How long was Sweeney out…
I'm getting' to that, don't worry, keep your fuckin' shorts on.

Anyway, someone pulled up to one of the public entrances down the beach a little. And I think it musta been them who called the Coast Guard, because it sure as hell wasn't me. And O'Dowd says it wasn't him either.

Sweeney's out there about another fifteen minutes, and in this time—I couldn't fuckin' believe it—the wind changed direction! It had been blowing onshore pretty hard in the morning when I'd checked it, and then the snow-squall thingy had happened and there wasn't much wind at all. I'm sitting there, watching, crouched on the mower's leather seat, and the wind picks up again—but from the west. By the time the third or fourth pulse shows on the horizon, it's blowing straight offshore at about eight or ten miles per hour. Unbelievable. I knew I was watching something fuckin' incredible goin' down.

The person who had pulled up to the public beach entrance had gone, so it wasn't Mike O'Dowd. He hadn't showed yet.

The next pulse comes in, and it looks huge. It looked like five feet bigger than everything else that day, so I thought it was going to close out like most of the other sets. And the first wave comes through and Sweeney lets it go—you don't want to take the first, fuck up, and get caught on the inside by the rest of the set. That's basic. Second and third waves are about the same size, and Sweeney lets them go. There's lines of swell out to the horizon, and the sun starts to peek out through the clouds. It doesn't come all the way through the clouds, not like some magic-halleluiah type shit, but it peeks through kinda dim and makes the water go completely silver. Kind of a dull grey-silver, with little whitish highlights. I'm getting' all Robert-Frost on ya, but like I said, fuckin' New England weather, right?

So the fourth and fifth and sixth waves come through and they close out from The Little Rocks to the rivermouth—just huge walls of silver feathering in the offshore breeze, and

Sweeney's paddling over each one, one by one. I'm standing on the seat of the mower, yelling, "Outside, outside you silly bastard!" or some such shit.

It must have been the tenth or eleventh wave of the set, it was fucking huge. I knew right away it was the one Sweeney was waiting for. He gets over the wave in front of it and just stops paddling. I can just see Sweeney like a speck sitting on the board facing the eleventh wave while getting rained on by the spray from the tenth wave pushed back by the offshore wind.

He's just sitting there. I'm like, "Paddle, paddle, you muthafuckahh! Go, go!" Sweeney just sits there until the thing's about to break on his head, then he spins the board around and pulls it under him with his black, gloved hand up near the yellow nose of the gun. He takes off at a sharp angle, he's going right, and doesn't even paddle. Not one stroke. Think about that shit!

This giant fuckin' wave comes all the way across the Atlantic, like eleventh in a set of what must've been fifteen waves, and Sweeney is out at just the right beach, and he's battled the rip and currents and closeout sets so that he's sitting in the exact right spot to take this wave. The fucking wave traveled a thousand miles just to pick him up from his little spot in the water. He didn't even paddle, just used the buoyancy of board to propel himself into this wave. It looked like he was slicing down a moving wall of, like, mercury or something, and it's feathering white at the top in the wind.

So he cuts down the steep face and the wave is already breaking above him, he's got his right hand out and it's dragging down the face behind him—leaving a little path like a skipping pebble behind him. I can see his white, bare feet on the deck of the board. They musta felt like bricks by then, nearly useless blocks on the end of your ankles after even ten minutes in that freezing water—nevermind the dusting of snow he just jogged through to get to the water!

He comes down into the trough of the wave, and he's gonna be deep in the barrel any second. He does a sort of half-bottom turn, and the last thing I see before the lip of the wave hides him from sight is a kick-stall. I mean, this wave is like fifteen- to eighteen-foot on the face, it's feathering down the line for about twenty or twenty five yards, and Sweeney pulls up under the lip and stalls a single fin. It's ridiculous. If you saw it, you'd say the same thing. While he's stalling, he's standing up straight, and I doubt he even had to crouch in that first barrel.

That barrel was the best and deepest ever ridden at Seawell, I don't give a flyin' fuck what anyone says about some swell back in 1969. With all due respect, those old-timers can go fuck themselves for all I care. This was the best barrel in New England's history. He was completely out of sight for a good eight or ten seconds, then he ducked under the end section of the barrel and came hauling out. He screams out onto the shoulder and throws a big, arcing carve. He knew how to ride that Hot Buttered like he had shaped the thing himself.

Sweeney carved the shoulder of that wave and then he sort of looked left and right and laid down on the Hot Buttered— back on his belly. The wave was just a ten-foot wall of whitewater at this point, and it was pushing him toward shore between The Little Rocks and Triangles. He starts angling left a little bit, still on his stomach, and then the wave starts to reform on the inside sandbar. Sweeney paddles a little bit, like two or three strokes, and then pops to his feet again and fades to the left and then bottom turns right on the frothy inside section. Little bits of foam are blowing out the back, and it looks like a snow squall coming off the lip of the wave. Sweeney bottom turns and carves up and down the face for speed about three or four times. He's flying across the Inside section in a low crouch, arms out, like, I've seen photos of Owl Chapman or somebody in the early '70s. Then he does an off-the-top and angles straight down the vertical face, right before the bowling section of Triangles. Usually Triangles is a wedgy A-frame that works mid- to high-tide, but when the waves are huge at Seawell it becomes a nasty, final, inside bowl section—one last, fat-lipped tube at the end of the wave. It breaks in only a few feet of water right there, kinda ugly and doubled-up a lot of the time, right near the rocks.

Sweeney comes down from the off-the-top, does a tiny fade to the left, and cranks a soul-arched bottom turn up under the thick lip that had been held up just long enough by the wind. He disappears again, in a crouch with his arms forward, for about four or five seconds. It musta been the second-best barrel ever at Seawell.

Well, maybe not, that's crazy-talk. But it was a deep, thick barrel and one of the best at Triangles in a long time.

He squeaked out of that one under the lip, just as the section in front of him was barreling right at him. He got clipped a little in the head by the lip, but he managed to stay on his feet, just barely. Then he just laid down again and rode the last twenty yards to ankle-deep water down in the corner of Seawell. He got out by the rocks at the rivermouth to my left.

Did Mike O'Dowd see it, did he show up in time?
No. I thought the guy was going to have to save Sweeney from drowning, but he drove up to one of the public entrances just as Sweeney came out of that second barrel. At least that's what he told me. By then, I couldn't take my eyes off Sweeney. I'm standing in silence on top of the riding mower's seat, hands in my pockets, shaking my head in fucking pure amazement.

Sweeney just waved up at me once, as he walked back down the beach and into the dunes. I don't know where the fuck he went. His clothes, the ones he went to jail in way back when, were in a pile back at my garage! I stopped wondering and I just went back to watching the ocean. I was freezing my ass off, but I waited for Mike to walk over from the public entrance, and then, just as he got to me, the Coast Guard and some TV crew showed up. They said they got a call about someone being pulled out to sea. They asked me if I'd seen anyone out there, and the Coast Guard guy had this worried look on his face as he pointed out toward another closeout set sweeping across the beach.

I told them you'd hafta be fuckin' loony to paddle out in that.

He says, "Paddle?"

I says, "Yeah, surfing in that shit's for the birds."

And me and Mike just laughed at the Coast Guard guy's confused look.

An' just then, the wind shifted to sideshore, outta the northeast, and blew the whole place back into the whitecapped, choppy mess it had been earlier that morning.

No word of a lie, I'm not even kidding.

"A LISTENING AIR…"*

I held the grit of the thick diving board
between my fingers. I was all-day drunk
and laid-out, fully clothed on a green raft.
Stan and I had pool-hopped on our walk from the bar
to "late-night" at our friend's mom's house in Rathmines.
It was nearly three o'clock in the morning in June,
and I'd found my slurred reverence for summer.

It's now late November,
five years later, and the trees
drop their dry hints of winter.
They pile and lie murmuring
against the dormant grass—
heaped syllables cast from a worn voicebox.
The beeches and black oaks
reserve a choice few—the rattling
stragglers of autumn.
The wind lisps, invisibly,
across the emptied canopies of Seawell
until I'm urged back,
reminded of that summer night.

I felt the grit of the white diving board
in my left hand as I dug through and sloshed
in submerged pockets. I threw Stan his dripping
ignition key. He drove to Twelfth and Bridge—
the Karnick's house, for late-night beer and noise.
I was left with the unrest of dialects—
a hushed breeze moved like a thrown voice through the willows.

Today, the bell-shaped dome
of remaining beech leaves
wanes to a skirt of yellowed bickering.
The clamor's wrung by the gusts,
just as leaf-green's wrung by the sun.

58

And I released the edge of the diving board
to measure the accent—foreign and obscure—
as it was tossed from tree to ragged tree.
A slackened, traceable, and clockwise wind
argued and gestured among the blown tufts
of dense foliage gone grey in the distance.
My wet head rested on its inflated pillow.
I spun, shadowless, and stared at the lush orations
of summer pushing me about the pool:
from deep to shallow, around low end to deep,
along white curbs—reckless near journeys in sleep.

—Sweeney

* Sweeney gave this poem to Gerald Francis in the clubhouse bar at
Farannan Golf Course in 1993 on the day Gerald turned 60. Sweeney
told Gerald that he lifted this poem's title from Robert Frost, Gerald's
favorite poet. The phrase originally appears in Frost's poem, "The Sound
of Trees."

Chapter 5

MISSION TO THE BOAT RANCH

Most of the stories in this collection appear in the order in which they came to me. Usually, an interview with an acquaintance of Sweeney's led me to the next interview; one person recommended talking to another and so on and so forth. This chapter, however, was the last I recorded. Once the storyteller, Sweeney's cousin Tommy Santos, told me the following story I realized that it needed to appear early on in the collection to help flesh out aspects of Sweeney's life.

As far as my second interview with Tommy, this is how it came about: Tommy called me up, but didn't sound good on the phone. He said he wanted to meet with me to tell me about "all the shit that happened in Mexico, all the shit that happened because of Pepperdine." We agreed to meet two days later, at The Nightjar, for an interview over breakfast before Tommy went off to work for the day. Tommy said to me, "Don't forget your tape recorder. You hafta hear this story. No one has heard this one, and it explains a lot about Sweeney goin' to jail and goin' crazy an' stuff like that."

But, the night before we were supposed to meet at the diner for this second interview, Tommy called me from the pay-phone in McSwiggans. He sounded pretty drunk. He asked me if I had a tape recorder that would work over the phone. I told him I did, but it wasn't set up. He said, "Okay, set it up. No, wait, wait. Hang up. Wait. Hang up after I tell you this, then set up the recorder thing and I'll call you right back. I gotta take a piss." He hung up.

I set up the recorder, but the phone never rang.

I went to The Nightjar Diner the next day, not knowing what to expect, and Tommy was waiting for me in a booth. He had a half-eaten bacon-egg-and-cheese sandwich in front of him, with two empty cans of Mountain Dew sitting on the table.

I started the recorder right after ordering my own breakfast.

Yah, sorry kid. I shoulda called you back last night, but Scotty Khim came in as I was takin' a piss. He bought me like three root-beer barrels. We useta play street hockey together when we were kids over in the Acre. I hadn't seen the guy in years. Anyways, I was *all done* after that. I was gonna call you, but I was fuckin' all done, kid.

Yeah, you don't look too good. Feelin' a little banged up?
Yah, no shit. But I wanna do this. I gotta go to work in about forty-five minutes, so I'll give you the revised version of this whole thing. My fuckin' wife will kill me if I don't get this off my chest. It's been buggin' me really bad since we last talked. Thanks for *that*, by the way.

Sorry, but I didn't know any…
Ahh, I'm just fuckin' with ya. Let's get goin' before your food gets here. You recording this yet?

Let me double-check…All set, go ahead.
Good. Yeah, so I told you I went down to Baja after Sweeney dropped outta Pepperdine. I think I mentioned that last time we talked? Anyways, I went down there with Sweeney's old high school girlfriend, Brigit Beaulieu. She was a real winner, let me tell you that. Traveling with her sucked. I never liked the girl, she never liked me, but she needed someone who could speak Spanish to help her find Sweeney in Baja.

You speak Spanish, Tommy?
No, I don't actually. I lied to her and my uncle. I speak a little Portuguese, my family's Portuguese. You'd think my uncle would've known that, huh? But he's an idiot, as you'll see. And I told Brigit I spoke Spanish because I wanted to go see Sweeney—see if I could get him back to Seawell. At least I thought I did, at the time.

See, I'm gonna hafta go to work, so, umm, I'm just gonna say this. You can take it for what it's worth.

Brigit and Uncle Jon, Sweeney's father, were real tight. Sweeney and Brigit weren't even going out anymore. That's what fuckin' pisses me off about all this; Sweeney didn't want anything to do with the girl at that point. But Brigit, in some twisted fuckin' way, thought that if she got Sweeney to come back to Seawell with her he would see that they were supposed to be together, that they belonged together or somethin'. She was about as fun as a bag of wet leaves, ya know? Usually, I steered clear of her.

Anyways, Brigit and Uncle Jon tell me to go out there and let Sweeney know that his mother, Diane, was sick and that they didn't think she would die, but that she was going to be in the hospital for a long time and she wanted to see him. Sweeney's mother had gone through a long stay in the hospital once when we were growing up. I think she had cystic fibrosis or something like that, I'm not sure. Whatever it was, they told me she was back in the hospital for the same thing. At the time they told me this, she was in the hospital but who knows what for. Coulda been a fuckin' hangnail, and I wouldn't-ah-known because I didn't really ask.

But, at the time, I said, ya know, since Sweeney's dad was asking me to help out, I said, "No problem, of course, whatever you need. Yeah, I speak Spanish..." and blah, blah, blah. I figured I could get by with my Portuguese. Uncle Jon'd never asked me for anything before, so I assumed that it must've been serious at the very least. I never saw Uncle Jon that much when we were growing up. Sweeney'd be the first to tell you his father was a prick—a real fuckin' brainwashed, military hardass. You know the sorta guy I mean. The thing was, he was never even in the military. He had some injury and they wouldn't let him in. He was a technical consultant for them, like high-tech missile technology or somethin'. But he played the part with how he raised Sweeney and treated my Aunt Diane. *[For more on Sweeney's family, see Appendix C.]*

Anyways, to make a long story short, I never got to go and visit Aunt Diane before I went out West. They told me she wasn't seeing visitors—a bunch of bullshit. Like two days later, I fly out there with Brigit. I'm tryin' to be all understandin' and helpful with the little lying cunt, ya know? She told me that her and Sweeney had been in touch the whole time he was out at Pepperdine. I just believed everything she said because I didn't know what the fuck was going on. I just knew we were supposed to go about five hours south, past Tijuana, past Ensenada to this little town of Jaramillo.

Look that up, because I have no idea how to spell it. Begins with j-a-r, I think.

In any case, Sweeney was supposed to be living down there. I was up for whatever, it didn't matter to me, I figured we'd find the guy somehow. Brigit told me she wanted to break the news to Sweeney, that it would be better that way. I was like, "Whatever. Do what you gotta do, this is a free vacation for me. Let's go get the bastard, let's drink some beers, get some Cuban cigars." All that shit, ya know? I was clueless. I think about it now, and I realize I had somehow managed to shove my big fat head all the way up my ass and I didn't really care.

Fuck, awwright, umm, how do I say all this? I can't be late for work today. I gotta get down to it.

Ahhhm, so, we meet up with some of Brigit's college friends up in Mission Beach in San Diego. This guy, Shane, says he'll take us down to Jaramillo because he seen Sweeney down there a couple weeks ago on a surf trip. Shane, actually, was an okay guy. He didn't drink that much with me, but I saw him surf and he was pretty fuckin' good. And, thank fuckin' god, he knew his way down to The Boat Ranch pretty well. I mean, he found the dirt road out of Jaramillo that pretty much went right to The Ranch, and they all looked the same to me down there. We woulda been lost without the guy.

So, somehow, it turns out that this guy that'd met Sweeney surfing back here in North Seawell was down at Cuatro Casas...

Wait, where's the place you're going again?
Oh, ahhhm, it's weird: The town is called Jaramillo and it's a couple miles inland from this surf spot called Cuatro Casas. It's down in the desert, the middle of nowhere. Right above the surf spot, on the cliffs, there's this collection of old, retired fishing boats up on stilts, or barrels or something—like, 25-foot trawlers and old lobster boats—and they're all arranged in this circle, kinda like a wagon train, but with boats.

And this guy, Shane—the guy driving us—met Sweeney

surfing in North Seawell when he was like sixteen. So he sees Sweeney down at Cuatro Casas randomly, staying at The Boat Ranch, that's what they call it. I guess this was like a couple weeks after Sweeney'd dropped outta Pepperdine. Shane talks to Sweeney and they figure out the connection, they smoke each other up, they drank a bunch of beers and they surf and Shane goes back to San Diego and tells some people, ya know, that he saw this random guy in Mexico that he met like ten years before in Seawell, Mass. He's just sorta telling the small-world-story thing to some people at a party in San Diego, you know what I mean? And, anyway, one of the girls he tells this story to thinks Sweeney might've been her friend Brigit's old boyfriend who visited up at the University of New Hampshire when her and Brigit were both freshmen there. She thought it sounded just like him, and she'd heard from Brigit that Sweeney had left Pepperdine and all that. It was fucked. Pretty random, ya know?

But, in any case, that's how Brigit found out where Sweeney was and she went straight to her favorite—my Uncle Jon. Sometimes, I think she liked Uncle Jon more than she liked Sweeney, but that's another story. Like I said, the two of 'em contacted me, and next thing I know me and Brigit are in an old, blue, beat-up, '83 Jeep Cherokee goin' down to The Boat Ranch.

Eventually, we get there and Sweeney fuckin' freaks out when he sees us. He was out in the water surfin', and we watched him from up on the cliff. Shane paddled out and told Sweeney we were there. We got a fire going on the edge of the cliff with some wood we brought, 'cuz Brigit thought it was getting a little cold. But it was nice out, man. Nothin' like Massachusetts-cold, ya know? Anyways, Sweeney looks up at us sitting in our beach chairs drinkin' Pacificos, and he waves—kind of confused and half-assed. He didn't know what to make of it. He took one or two more waves, and then he came out. Shane didn't know anything about Sweeney's father bein' sick, I mean Sweeney's mother, but Sweeney came out of the water kind of knowing that we were there to bring him back to Seawell for whatever reason. So we go up to Sweeney and he's psyched to see us, he's still in his wetsuit, dripping in the dirt. He's psyched, but he's like, "What the fuck are you guys doing here?"

Brigit blurts out, "Oh, Shane knows such-an-such-a-friend-of-mine and they talked and figured out that you were down here and she called me and I talked to Tommy," and she just bullshit him, you know? Sayin' something like: "and we just wanted to come and visit and say hi."

I knew something was going wrong there, but I wasn't sure what. I was drunk, I didn't really care. I remember I was pissing right there off the cliff as I turned back to Sweeney when she finished blabbing, and I was like, "Yeah, Sweeney, I'm Brigit's official translator and guide, Tommy Santos. How ya been? Nice to meet you." I had a cigar in my mouth, pissin', I was just bein' a wise ass. I was like, "You know you can drink in the car in this country? I love this fuckin' place. Beautiful country. Now, tell me, *amigo*, where the fuck are the beers?" I was tanked from drinking since Ensenada.

Turns out my Spanish, or Portuguese, wasn't needed at all since Shane drove us right to the spot. That bein' the case, I decided I'd have a few road sodas as we left Ensenada. I was about eight beers deep when we got to The Ranch. Sweeney was laughin' at me.

So I guess Brigit put off telling Sweeney about his father or mother being sick at that point, because we all got drunk that first night, except for Shane. He wanted to surf in the morning, so he just smoked us all up and went to bed kinda early. He had some crazy fuckin' chronic stuff. It was good weed, but he wouldn't touch a beer. Kinda weird, but whatever. So he goes off to one of the boats to sleep and me and Brigit and Sweeney sat around the fire pit until like two in the morning, and we were throwin' down Pacificos like they were goin' outta style. Good fuckin' beer, too—with a slice of lime stuck in the neck. I'll drink those fuckin' things all night, but not too many bars around here have 'em.

Anyways, the next morning it was hot as fuck in the boat I had passed out in. It was comfortable all night until that desert sun hit it around eight. Those boats are great, way better than sleeping in some tent in the dirt. They're all teakwood and clean and they have all these different sized beds in 'em with those

Mexican blankets and stuff. I even found a big old bed for a fat bastard like myself.

But, that morning, I wake up sweatin' like a freak. I stumble out and down the ladder of my boat. I went across The Ranch to take a piss out behind one of the boats. It was named the Ronnie Brosnan, he was some surfer from the '50s or '60s, if I remember right. Whoever set up the place had it dialed, there were bottle openers bolted to the hulls of the boats so you could open a Pacifico wherever you walked. I remember I cracked open the first of the day on the hull of one of the boats, and then I went behind the side of the boat next to it to take a piss. They had a pipe with a giant oyster shell, or some kind of shell, stuck to the top of it with a drain in the center of it so you could piss and it would go down to a real septic system. It was a crazy, fuckin' cool place. Sweeney told me he named all the boats after famous surfers—The Duke, The Skip Frye, and a bunch of others. He painted the names on there himself.

So, I'm there pissing and I hear Brigit start yelling something. I'm like, "Ohh fuck, here we go."

I'm rollin' my eyes, and then I hear Sweeney say, "Well, whaddyamean you don't know what 'exactly' he's sick with? You came all the way down here and...and blah, blah, blah," you know?

I was still sorta groggy from the night before, but I remember bein' like, "He? Why would Sweeney be asking about Uncle Jon?" I'm standing there with my prick hanging out, it's like 8:30 in the morning, I'm drinking my one-thousandth Pacifico of the trip and I'm as fuckin' confused as I've ever been in my life. I just sort of paused, and then I shrugged it off and tried to go back to sleep for a little bit. It didn't work, it was hot as hell in the boat and then by like 9:15 Sweeney had us all running around cleaning up The Ranch and getting ready to leave.

When he was locking up the boats and the big iron gate, and me and Brigit and Shane are sitting in the car waiting to go, I says to Brigit, "What the hell did you tell him?"

She fuckin' hemmed and hawed and was like, "Umm, I figured that umm, he would be too upset if I told him it was his mother that was sick, so I told him it was his father. He hates his father, so I thought he wouldn't be..."

I didn't even let her finish, I was like, "Brigit you are a certifiable fucking nutcase. You are a lying sack of shit. I mean it. I don't know what the fuck is goin' on here, but you are full of shit and I want no part of it."

I just kinda knew something was fundamentally wrong with whatever was going on.

She begged me to keep quiet during the ride, and I was, again, tyin' one on, so I told Sweeney, I lean out the window and I'm like, "Bro, I don't know what the fuck is going on right now, but your parents want you to come home and we gotta get the fuck outta Dodge." I think Sweeney might've thought I was just rehashing the obvious, so he sorta ignored me and just gave me a shut-the-fuck-up-Tommy look.

I was familiar with that look. It was a tense ride home— from what I remember of it, anyway. I was bugging Sweeney about how he fucked up his free ride at Pepperdine and shit like that, but he wasn't even listening to me. I mean, how do you fuck up a free lunch like that? Seriously, you know?

But he wasn't listening and no one wanted to stop into Hussong's in Ensenada for some more beers, despite my reasoning. Then the Mexican army guys, the Federales, searched our car like three times for drugs or guns or whatever. I do remember pissing in a Gatorade bottle a few times while sharing the backseat with Brigit. It was a long drive, ya know? That was pretty good. She wasn't happy. No one was happy. I think Shane, the poor kid, thought we were a bunch of lunatics. He didn't say much on the drive home.

Ahhh, shit! Look at the fuckin' time, I gotta run. Here's the deal, in a nutshell:

Brigit *and* Uncle Jon had lied to me so I would help get Sweeney back to Seawell. I finally found out Aunty Diane wasn't seriously ill, it was like a compound fracture in her leg that needed some pins put in. So when we got to Baja, Brigit told Sweeney his Dad was sick because she knew not to really mess with Aunty Diane. Uncle Jon didn't give a fuck about lying to me or to

Sweeney, he just didn't approve of his son's decision to leave Pepperdine and so he set up the whole fucking thing to get Sweeney back home. A recon mission. I mean, what an asshole— ya know?

And then there's me? I was just a stupid, drunk fuck who went along for the ride. Sweeney, like I said before, was not happy with me. He really didn't even ask me what was going on with his sick father while we were coming back here because I told him I was clueless and didn't want to be involved. I guess I was okay with dragging him back to Seawell because, back then, I was sorta pissed at him for screwing up Pepperdine and giving up baseball and shit like that. I mean, I guess I didn't have a right to be pissed or whatever, it probably wasn't any of my business. At least, that's what my wife keeps telling me. But I was pissed— like a lot of us that grew up with Sweeney, playing baseball with him and stuff. And I was drunk almost the whole time I was on the West Coast, so I told Sweeney to just talk to Brigit about all of the family shit that was going on. I was drinking *a lot* back then, I don't remember all of it.

Later, after we got back to Seawell, I was pleading my innocence with him, but I kinda knew I'd let him down.

Sweeney came back to Seawell, then went straight to Rhode Island to see his supposedly-on-his-deathbed father. He got there and all was well and his mother was in a cast, happier than hell to see him. Sweeney finally talked to his mother and found out she didn't even know that we'd gone to Baja to get him. And she couldn't even tell him who was lying about what! She was the only one more clueless than me in the whole thing— pretty fuckin' sad situation, when I think about it now.

Needless to say, Sweeney flipped out on his father and swore he'd never talk to him again because he couldn't ever trust him. He barely talked to the guy anyway, so it wasn't too much of a change. Then he came back to work for Goatboy to try to save more money to go traveling again. His mother, although she loved Sweeney and never forgave Uncle Jon for what he did, she stayed with that stupid prick of a husband and they moved far- ther south to, like, Baltimore or somewhere a few months later. I don't think Sweeney talked to them much anymore. I don't even know where they are now, and they're my aunt and uncle—well, Aunty Diane is sisters with my real uncle's wife. So Sweeney's like my third cousin or something. I'm not sure how it works, really, maybe he's once-removed or some such shit?

But by that point, Sweeney wanted to kill Brigit. I mean, seriously. I think he seriously thought about killing her. And Brigit, she was just miserable, just a bad person—she claimed she didn't understand why anyone was mad at her. She actually had the fuckin' gall to say to me once, "But nobody understands that Sweeney and I are soulmates!" I contemplated killing her myself, to be honest.

Sweeney made her and me swear we wouldn't tell anyone about the whole fuckin' fiasco. That was the first thing he did when he came back from Rhode Island, when he'd figured it all out. I kept up my end of the deal until now, talkin' to you. Brigit, once she got it through her thick head that Sweeney was never going to talk to her again, just moved to Colorado or Idaho. She just got outta here, which was the best thing for everyone involved I think. She was gone in the span of about two or three months after Sweeney was back in Seawell.

Then, like I told you [in Chapter 8], Sweeney got a little mean, ended up clocking that Mormon kid and wound up out at Merritt for a couple years or so. He and I were never really that close again. He came out of Merritt and a little while later he stole the ice cream truck and they put him out at Darville. Who the fuck knows what he's done since then, really, ya know?

I mean, seriously, the guy went crazy after a while. Who could blame him with a father like that, and a mother who won't stand up for herself? Don't get me wrong, I love my Aunty Diane and Sweeney, but things were fucked up over there too. I certainly don't blame Sweeney, he never really had a family that took care of him or anything—nothing to fall back on like most of us.

But, like I said before, I just really wish I'd done things differently back then—laid off the sauce, paid a little attention to the shit that was going on, ya know? I fucked up, big-time. I guess I still don't understand how Sweeney just walked away from his baseball scholarship either. That's kinda shitty of me, I know, but me and a lot of people in Seawell can't forgive him for wasting his ticket outta this place. Probably stupid to still let that shit bother me, but it does.

And, on top of all that shit, now I'm late for work.

Wait! Does anyone else knows about this, like Goatboy or my father?

Trust me, kid, no one else knows about this one unless Sweeney told 'em, 'cuz I sure as hell didn't tell anybody. Your father asked me about it once, I think. But I didn't want to talk about it, so I got pissed at him for asking and just mouthed-off about the Pepperdine thing and called Sweeney a quitter. But Brigit's out in Colorado somewhere just bein' the bitch that she is, so she hasn't been talking to many people around here. No one would believe her anyways, everyone's had their fill of her. Mostly, I've been too freakin' ashamed to even bring the whole thing up— I mean, I eventually told my wife but that was like four or five years after it all happened.

Speakin' of my wife, she'll be glad to hear I told you all this. She thinks I'm not really to blame here, and I hope, now that I've gotten all this shit off my chest, I might be able to figure out what I did wrong. I mean, I *know* what I did wrong, but maybe now I can start to feel a little bit better about all of it. Who knows? We'll see how it goes.

I gotta run, here's twenty for breakfast. Keep the change. See ya later, and I hope I never see you again you fuckin' inquisitive bastard. You're like the goddamned therapist I never had *(Laughs to himself as he leaves)*.

MIGUELITO

lies splayed in the schoolyard and cranes
his dusty head—a bony fist
clenching sentience and old brains.
His jaw dips in stale sand, some grist
for the mill of his mouth. His shell is burnished
by the kids' leanings: rough grey to black,
the shine stands, permanently polished
on the dome of his ancient back.
His slow lurch, wisest of animals
in the yard, heaves his dark bulk—the most
adored but harried of pet mammals.
He strains. If he could speak, he would boast
of his century's worth of years,
knowing it's the widest breadth of time
our fast but feeble minds might hear
and grasp. Later he'd describe the crime:
Demented, mass slaughter that's clear-
cut through all species of common sense.
His kind nearly extinct, he fears
our kind—the fast and feeble—in silence.
He snaps at the fluttering, soft pass
of a hand, inches back, tramps dead grass.
The globed breadth of his rockhard shell
holds a wolf moon in its hidden well—
his flesh-dense haven and hollow hell.

—Sweeney

* For the resident Galapagos Tortoise
at *La Escuela de Miguel Valverde*, Bahía de Caraquez

(Scrawled in tiny cursive writing on a postcard with a picture of a gigantic, menacing statue of The Virgin Mary overlooking the city of Quito,
Ecuador, 1997.)

Chapter 6

YARDBIRD AND THE GEEZERS

This chapter is culled from several interviews with Margaret Tierney, lifelong member at Farannan Golf Course. Margaret taught fourth grade at Oakland Elementary School for thirty-five years, was an avid tennis player and golfer when she was younger, and now resides at Fairheath Nursing Home in Pentucketville. Most importantly, Margaret was a friend and mentor for Yardbird Sweeney when he was a child. She was more than happy to reminisce about a young Sweeney, and she told me that she hopes Sweeney will return to Seawell someday and maybe even visit her at Fairheath.

Margaret is a self-described "dowdy old bird" with grey curls framing a friendly, smiling, oval face. She reminded me of more than a few elementary school teachers I had when I was younger. I didn't have to ask Margaret many questions, she began talking, pausing only to sip at one of her many cups of tea, and she told me all she cared to remember.

I first knew Yardbird when he was just a little thing, running around the course all day long. He was always sunburned and muddy, and he was a quite an alert boy. He really wouldn't say much unless you goaded him into a conversation. Now, what I remember is that he loved to hunt for golf balls in the ponds on eight and nine and in the out-of-bounds woods off four, six and seven. He'd be in and out of the woods all day. Once in a while, I'd see him up in the seaside blackthorn near the green on four. He just sat there in the limbs, peacefully watching all the foursomes approach the green to play out the hole. He'd wave to some of the golfers that he knew, others he'd let pass without a sound or any movement to give away his aerie. His tanned legs would be dangling slowly, mud drying from deep brown to a sort of clay color on the soles of his bare feet. Even back then he was difficult to find. He never wore white or yellow or the type of clothing that would attract attention in the bright green canopy during the summer months. He always wore khaki shorts and a forest green or navy blue T-shirt. And you know, come to think of it, I don't believe I ever saw the child wear socks. Most of the children wore knee-high tube socks back then around Seawell, knee-high tube socks and, oh, what's their name? Those red high-top shoes. . .Chuck Taylors. Yes, that's it, Chuck Taylors. But little Yardbird never wore socks and he always had flip-flops or went barefoot. He was the picture of summer with his mussed, dark brown hair, tan face and light freckles scattered across his cheek-bones. If he wanted you to know he was around, he would take his flip-flops out of his back pocket, slip them on and start walk-ing toward you along the edge of a fairway. Otherwise, he was nearly impossible to find. He really was a fixture on that course; I believe he lived in a little split-level Ranch with his parents on Yewtree Avenue—past the woods on the right of number three, so whenever the weather was nice he could be found somewhere on that course.

One summer, he must have been five or six, I started teaching him about the trees at Farannan. It was just after I saw him coming up off the beach behind the green on number seven one day in June. I'd never really talked to the boy at that point; I'd only watched him enjoying his summer days all around the course. He always waved to me when I saw him, because I golfed regularly in the summers back then, but we'd never spoken. But that day in June I watched him wash the mud from his shins and knees in the receding foam of the little waves beyond seven's green, and then he trotted back up the sand toward the green, flip-flops in hand. I waited for him, and he was a little shy, but he climbed up the rocks and onto the back fringe of the green. I had a few twigs from the hazelbirch over by number six and I offered him one to chew on. I told him my name, and he said his name was Sweeney. I said, "Sweeney? That's a nice Irish name, but don't you have a first name? My name's Tierney, and I'm Irish, too. My first name is Margaret, so you can call me Margaret."

I'd grown tired of the habit all the men in Seawell had of calling one another only by their last names. If you referred to any of the many unrelated Sullivan's by their first name there was mass confusion, but if you said "Sully, you know, the other Sully." everyone somehow knew who you meant. I tried to get Sweeney to tell me his first name, but he wouldn't tell me.

Later, I was to find out—and I found this very odd—his parents had named him Sweeney O'Sweeney. At least, that was the name on his birth certificate. What the *havill* would make his father and mother do that to their only child? I found out from Sweeney about a year after I'd met him. He was very embarrassed about his name, almost ashamed. He made me promise I wouldn't tell anyone his real name. I kept my promise, but I suppose it's all right that I've told you all these years later. Poor child, his parents were a little loopy from what I gathered—a little touched in the head, I'd say.

However, back to my story about the day we met. What Sweeney did tell me the first time we met was, "Some of the old men around here call me 'Yardbird.' I like that name. Mr. Francis says I'm like a junkyard dog, but with eyes like a hawk."

So Yardbird took the twig I offered and looked at it thoughtfully, then watched me chewing on my own hazelbirch twig. For a moment, I thought he didn't trust me, but then he smelled the wintergreen. He had striking green eyes, even as a boy, and he just looked at me and those eyes flashed as the taste hit his tongue. The simple fact that he could safely chew on a part of a tree without getting sick made his face light up. He was amazed that I knew all about plants and trees. I've been a gardener all my life, I love plants more than people sometimes. In any case, that little boy loved to learn about any flower or tree that New England had to offer. I told him to be careful not to call the old men around the course "old men." I told him to be sure to call them "geezers, as in 'Mr. Geezer, sir.' And you can tell them I told you that." He twisted up his face, a little confused, but then he nodded.

I laughed a little at his expressions, and told him to meet me by the seaside blackthorn the next Tuesday if he wanted to learn about the tree he was chewing on. Now, by the time he was eight or nine, I'm sure he knew all the trees and flowers that grew on the course by name. He loved to point out the slenderelf mushrooms, amanita muskbush, cork elder and coyote elder. He was a bright young boy, and polite and as nice as could be. You could tell that he was brought up properly—despite his family's other oddities. Sweeney minded all his manners and respected his elders and so on—elders of all kinds, both trees and people, I might add!

He was there, that next Tuesday. In fact, he had already climbed up about fifteen feet off the ground and was swinging his bare legs around in the branches of the seaside blackthorn, just waiting for me to tell him all about the tree.

The first thing Yardbird Sweeney ever learned about trees was how hazelbirch twigs, when you snapped them off, smelled of wintergreen. He was so happy that he could identify and name a tree by looking at the shape and color of the leaves and the direction of the "scrape marks" on a tree's bark. That's what he called the markings on a tree trunk. He'd say something like, "That one has a lot of flaky bark with up-and-down scrape-marks, and big leaves with five tips each. It's a shagsap maple. And this one, the one you can chew on the twigs, has side-to-side scrape marks that kinda look like a million eyeballs. It's a speck-led hazelbirch." From about age five to eleven, I don't believe I ever saw the boy without a hazelbirch twig hanging from the cor-ner of his mouth.

Each day, there he'd be, his face peeking out from the blackthorn leaves as I'd approach Tuesday mornings with my women's league foursome, and Saturday afternoons with the men's twilight league. It got to the point where I'd almost forget about playing some of the holes, instead trailing the other women and men while talking to him about the plants and trees and birds and animals on the course. Almost every Tuesday and Saturday he'd be waiting with four or five twigs for me and a few for himself, along with some wild bogberries, or bits of brine let-tuce from the tide pools. We'd stroll along together, pointing out trees and birds, and every once in a while I'd drop a ball and ask Sweeney what club I should use. He'd always stare intently in the direction of the hole, shade his eyes with both his hands, chew on his bottom lip, then say, "I think you need a seven iron," or whatever it was that he thought I needed.

And wouldn't you know it! He'd be right. I'd say, "Sweeney, my goodness, how did you know what club I needed? You always know."

He'd just smile and say something observant. Many

times, it was very simple, like "Margaret, the wind is blowing wicked hard in your face." Or, "Well, your ball didn't pass that Earcain yew yet, Margaret."

He picked it all up as quick as could be. We met every Tuesday and Saturday of every summer for years at that same seaside blackthorn. He'd walk with me and fore caddy, because he had strong eyes. I'd say he had abnormally strong eyes, stronger than any child I'd ever known. I'm not sure I ever lost a ball when he walked the course with me. All the old-geezer golfers loved Yardbird, they'd pay him a dollar and he'd go and find their ball and three more to go along with the one they originally duck-hooked into the woods. I believe, if I remember correctly, now, that was where the nickname "Yardbird" came from. He had eyes like a hawk, and he hung around that course like it was his own backyard, like a junkyard...have I already mentioned that? Am I repeating myself? I'm sorry, but it was such a curious nickname. And it stuck—like most curious nicknames do, whether you want them to or not.

I once saw him dive in the pond after a ball, this was when he was a little older, around ten or eleven. God's honest truth. I saw him go after one of those geezer's damned orange balls one day in August. It was Gerald Francis' ball, he was always the nicest to Sweeney out of all the old golfers at Farannan. Gerald duffed it into the water off of nine tee that day, just as I was coming off of eight, through the tunnel under two tee, to play number nine.

Sweeney was carrying Gerald's bag that day, as he sometimes did on Saturdays back then. There were no real caddies at Farannan, but Sweeney carried bags or fore caddied for his friends when he was bored with hunting for frogs and turtles in the ponds. We'd buy him a hot dog, or a lunch of some kind to pay him.

In any case, back to the lost ball. Sweeney started toward the water after Gerald's ball, all the frogs splashed out of sight as he kicked off his flip-flops and took off his green T-shirt. Gerald yelled at him, yelled something to discourage him. But Sweeney wouldn't listen, he wouldn't let the ball go. I remember I yelled at him, too: "Yardbird Sweeney, you will not go swimming in that pond after that ball. It's filthy in there. Do you hear me?" But Sweeney just looked back a little apologetically as he waded in through a smattering of terrified frogs, swam out to the middle and dove for the bottom. There was no visibility along the edge of that pond at two feet deep, never mind ten or twelve feet deep. It was half mud, half water by that point in the summer!

Sweeney must've been underwater for a good minute. I know it was this long, because the foursome from the first green stopped putting and came over—the Underhills, I believe. And it's a bit of a walk from the far side of the first green to the other side of the pond in front of nine tee.

I was very worried. I remember I started in the water after him. In fact, that's right, I remember now! I waded in up to my knees, worried sick, right there in my spikes and socks. Then the little menace popped up in the middle of the pond with a huge smile on his face and Gerald's orange ball raised over his head. He was triumphant, and that foursome of geezers let up a cheer they usually reserved for Red Sox games on the television in the bar.

All Sweeney said, as I glared at him from my soaked golf shoes was, "It was a Pinnacle-three, right Mr. Geezer, sir?" Those old men, the Underhills, and I all had a good laugh then. He was dripping wet, with that shining tan skin in the sun, standing on the gravel cart path in front of nine tee. He was such a nice child, really. Not a bad thing I can say about that boy back then. He was almost like a son to me and a few of the geezers at that course.

Now, as he got older, things were different. From what I hear, I believe he started hanging around with the wrong crowd. This was during the summers after his family had moved to Rhode Island. I believe Sweeney was around sixteen or so when his family decided to move to a town in Rhode Island, it might have been Providence. I believe his father was in the Navy, and was transferred from the old Seawell base down to a newer Rhode Island base. Now that I think about it, I suppose it was Narragansett. Yes, it was. However, Yardbird had become sort of a fixture in Seawell and he wasn't willing to give that up. He was a wonderful baseball player, I believe he was the catcher or the second baseman, in fact. I used to read all about him in the papers. He really was an above-average athlete. He had also become quite the surfer, so I hear, though I never really saw him surf much myself. I did see him play golf a few times, and I would say that he had a better natural swing than anyone else at Farannan in those years. Really, he excelled at whatever he put his mind to. I know that no one at Farannan wanted him to leave for Rhode Island. Everyone from the geezers to the groundskeepers offered him summer work so that he could come back when school was out.

I'm not sure what happened, but Yardbird never really left with his family. He remained enrolled at Seawell High School, partially due to the efforts of the baseball coach, I seem to recall. I think there was a falling out between Sweeney and his parents at that point in his life, and I don't think a boy of fifteen or sixteen should go through such a thing with his parents—not at that age. I'm willing to guess that was the time when Sweeney began to go astray.

I don't believe his grades or the athletics suffered too much. We talked about school here and there on the course, and it all came easily to him. Often, I had to discourage him from skipping class to go and read at the Public Library. He said he would rather read poetry and philosophy than sit through a Trigonometry class. I understood perfectly. I, myself, hate math and remember how tedious those classes could be. But I tried to instill in him the importance of good attendance—to no avail, I'm sorry to say. And I think that the lack of supervision during these years, until Sweeney went off to college, hurt him in the long run. I mean to say, after his parents left, we saw less and less of the boy on the course in those years. He always said he was working to pay rent and so forth, but he finally simply stopped appearing at Farannan during the day. Occasionally, someone would spot him surfing off the beach behind the seventh green, or the geezers would be mumbling about how he lived in the out-of-bounds area off number six, but he was no longer playing golf, or even keeping in touch with Gerald Francis any longer. He apparently was still doing some tree work for the greenskeeper, the "Goatman" or whatever the havill they call him. But that work was done during the early morning hours before the golfers swarmed the course, and I hardly ever saw him.

Some of us were worried, but teenagers are teenagers, as they say. What can one do in a situation like that? In a selfish way, I suppose I missed his company and I was upset about it a little bit. At that time, I must've been in my fifties when he was fifteen or sixteen. Any middle-aged woman in her right mind would've been a little miffed after losing the attention and friendship of such a nice young man.

In hindsight, and that seems to be the strongest sight I have these days, it really was a selfish attitude for me to take up. Maybe I could've helped him a little more through that troubled time in his life. Instead, I just imagined it was all part of being a teenager, that it was all part of something I shouldn't meddle with.

OBITUARY

Boris is dead. The fatalist parrot
No longer screams warnings to Avenue A.
He died last week on a rainy day.
He is sadly missed. His spirit was rare.

The cage is empty. The unhooked chain,
His pitiful droppings, the sunflower seeds,
The brass sign, "Boris," are all that remain.
His irritable body is under the weeds.

Like Eliot's world, he went out with a whimper;
Silent for days, with his appetite gone,
He watched the traffic flow by, unheeding,
His universe crumbling, his heart a stone.

No longer will Boris cry, "Out, brief candle!"
Or "Down with tyranny, hate, and war!"
To astonished churchgoers and businessmen.
Boris is dead. The porch is a tomb.
And a black wreath decorates the door.

by Weldon Kees

from *The Collected Poems of Weldon Kees* (Revised Edition),
    Edited by Donald Justice, University of Nebraska Press, Lincoln and
    London, 1975.

OBITUARÍO

Boris es muerto. El loro fatalisto
No puede gritar los avisos a La Avenida de A.
Se murío en la semana pasada durante un día lluvioso.
El esta anhelado con tristeza. Su alma fue rara.

La jaula esta vacía. La cadena separada,
Su guano pitiable, las semillas de girasol,
La señal del latón, "Boris," son todo que permanecer.
Su cuerpo iracundo esta debajo de las malas hierbas.

Como al mundo de Eliot, salío con un lloriqueo;
En silencio para algunos días; no tenía hambre,
Miraba el flujo del tráfico, sin interés,
Su universo se caía pedazos, su corazón como una piedra.

Boris no gritará más, "¡Apague, la candela breve!"
O "¡Maldiga la tiranía, el odio y la guerra!"
A la gente asombrada desde la iglesia y los hombres de negocios pasmados.
Boris es muerto. El pórtico es un tumba.
Y una corona negra decora la puerta.

—"Obituary," by Weldon Kees, translated by Sweeney

(Mailed to Patrick Kivlin along with the original English version from
Huatulco, Mexico, 1992.)

Chapter 7

THE GUN HEIST

The following is a letter written at my request by Sweeney's high school teammate and friend, Peter "The Wizzah" Joyce. It was typed on onionskin paper, on an old typewriter that was apparently missing the letter "r." I've fixed that and a few spelling errors but, other than that, I've reproduced it here without changes. It offers a little insight into some of the places Sweeney visited during the years he was in and out of Seawell after he'd gone to jail and Darville Mental Hospital. Peter, the author, believes the following story happened in the winter of '95-'96, I lean more toward the belief that it was '96-'97. Sweeney was approximately 26 or 27 years old.

Dear Owen,

How's things? I decided to answer your request for a Sweeney story because it sounds like no one has ever put down on paper the whole "gun heist" incident from a few winters ago. I know you wanted me to write this out, for whatever reason, but I'm not that good at writing letters or stories or anything like that. So I decided to go to the bar with some friends from work and a tape recorder. We whacked back a couple pitchers to warm me up and then I told them a long story. A couple weeks later I got around to listening to the recording and typing it all out exactly as I told it. I figured that was the best way to let you know how Sweeney got a hold of his favorite surfboard, but it took me way longer than I originally thought it would.

Irregardless, I hope it helps you figure some shit out about that guy. Tell him Wizzah says what's up when you see him, and if he wants to come back out to work as a liftie I've got a job waiting for him.

—Pete

"I'm not sure I should even be telling you clowns any of this, but here goes. It's a long one. It all went down a few years after Sweeney went to jail for that brawl in Sun Valley in north Seawell. He did about two years at Merritt and then spent a couple years after that acting a bit feral. He stole an ice cream truck and they diagnosed him as Schizophrenic or something like that, and put him in Darville Mental for a while.

"Then it was about two or three winters after they let him out of Darville that Sweeney wanted out of Seawell. He'd had his share of winter surf at the points in North Seawell. It had never gotten as good as we had it that fall during the swell from that No-Name Storm a couple years before. Those were the best waves Seawell will ever see—clean and long and empty—like an East-Coast Rincon, just epic for Seawell. Sweeney made the call to move to the mountains for a season before hitting up Orange County for a quiver of surfboards and then on to Central America—at least that's what he told me he was going to do. He'd always wanted to dedicate a winter to hiking for deep powder, but the surf bug had always kept him searching elsewhere.

"I played baseball with Sweeney at Seawell High, and Sweeney knew I was running the lifts at a certain mountain resort, that shall remain nameless, in the Sierra Nevadas. I offered him a job as a liftie and he took it. He got out there in early November and I put him on the easiest schedule imaginable—three, sometimes four, days a week. I didn't need the help, really, but I knew Sweeney didn't want to start spending whatever money he already had stashed for his upcoming trips. The salary covered rations and beer, and me and Sweeney usually spent the other three or four days of the week hiking around the backcountry by ourselves. It was one of the infamous El Niño winters and the Sierra Nevadas were getting pounded with snow. We scored our fill of fresh powder that year, my friends.

"Lookit, the second week he's out there Sweeney stopped into one of the upper-mountain lodges for a beer—and he rarely, if ever, spent any time or money in those damn places. The snow was still a little thin in early November, so Sweeny'd been sticking to the resort's trails at that point, just exploring and figuring out where they all went. So he goes into the lodge and heads back toward the bar. He passed by the cafeteria grill and that's when he first saw it—his magic surfboard. The thing was fucking perfect: a pristine, red dye-job with a pinstripe outline of yellow on the deck. It looked like a late, rare, Ronnie Brosnan-shaped Pipeline board.

"Ronnie was this California guy who first went over to Hawaii when he was real young, back in the late '40s, and went back every winter for years and years. Eventually, Brosnan was living out by Honolua Bay in a tool shed by himself. The guy was a trip. He didn't like the scene that was just starting up on the North Shore or anywhere else in the islands. He liked surfing alone, or with a few Hawaiian locals. The locals at Honolua say he had that place wired. It's a long, hollow right—like a point wave, off these cliffs, that can hold some size. They say he could ride it at any size and make it look easy. He just lived up off the point in a shack and grew pineapples and dove for sea turtles and spearfished. There's this sort of story about how he only showed up on the North Shore for the biggest swells. He'd always just be there, one of the only guys to paddle out when it was 20-foot and bigger. He rode these long balsa-wood big-wave boards he shaped for himself out behind his shack. He'd developed his shapes through pure trial and error. Wouldn't ride anything else, only his own. Only a few foam boards made by his hand exist. He said he never liked foam, just wood—something about riding a board that was once a living entity. I admire his aesthetics, so did Sweeney. Although, we've all been riding mostly foam boards pretty much since we started surfing back in Seawell.

"So there's Sweeney in an imitation Bavarian upper-mountain lodge in the Sierra Nevadas staring at a Ronnie Brosnan down-rail seven-foot-six.

"He told me all about that first moment, that love-at-first-sight thing. He had to have the damn thing. It didn't belong in some inland cafeteria, hung in the greasy glow of a fryolater. He was enthralled and enraged all at once, standing there staring at his magic board, three feet above his head. He told me we had to bring it back to the sea. He wanted to drop into some double-overhead bombs on that thing. The question was how to get his hands on it. I caught him whispering to himself once while we were drinking at The King's Head one night. I called him on it and he was like, 'Fuck you, Wizzah, I have to calm myself down somehow, so I keep telling myself, "The board isn't going anywhere. It isn't going anywhere."'"

"I'd been at the resort four or five years by that point. I knew everyone and everyone knew me. Sweeney came to me right away—the guy from his hometown who useta get in trouble with him after school an' shit. And out there, outside of Seawell, I'd managed a level of notoriety by getting fucking hammered every weekend, crashing on someone's couch and then sleep-walking wasted around whatever apartment I was in. There were a couple times where I'd forgotten to check the location of the bathroom before passing out, and there'd been a few times where I'd pissed on a houseplant or in someone's sock drawer. The best story is the one where I pissed on this snowboarder chick's plaid dogbed and the dog had it out for me. Sweeney heard a few stories and started calling me 'The Wizzer.' It caught on, but no one pronounced it that way because they all loved Sweeney's diehard Seawell accent—so they all called me 'The Wizzah.' It was funny as shit, and I didn't care either way, whatever. A nickname's a nickname, and there was no way of getting around the fact that I'd done my best impression of a sprinkler in a few living rooms back in those days.

"But, yeah, anyway, Sweeney came to see me about the Brosnan shape. I told him it was owned by the manager of the place at that time, Gene Perkins. Gene grew up in the Inland Empire in Orange County, California, and his dad handed the board down to him like 20 years ago when Gener was just a little kid. Gener never even tried the thing in any real surf, rumor has it, because he said 'the water was too cold in the winter.' He just put the poor thing up in the rafters of his garage when he was a kid. I heard that he only took it out at Doheny once or twice or something like that, and he'd already turned down all offers to buy it. I'd offered Perkins some good money myself, actually. Right then, when he heard all this, Sweeney nearly lost his shit. He flipped. I was laughing at him, he was so fucking pissed.

"I was laughing pretty hard, so Sweeney told me that if I didn't shut up and help him come up with a plan to get that board back to the ocean he'd tell every gaper and liftie on the mountain that I shit myself once on New Year's back in Boston when we were walking home from the bars. I was like, 'Jesus

Christ, Sweeney, shut the hell up. I'll help you. What the fuck's your problem?'

"I mean, the guy could be a prick if he wanted to. Lookit, I didn't care if he told everyone about that night. I had to take a dump and I slipped on some ice on the damn sidewalk, a little came out. I was wasted, it was New Year's, big deal. You know? Who gives a fuck? I told him I was planning on sneaking back into that snowboarder chick's place and squatting a grumpy on that stupid dog's bed anyways. Sweeney laughed his ass off at that one, and then we started coming up with a plan to relieve Gene Perkins of his treasure.

"We waited until it was deep. Real deep. By January there had been like eight huge dumps up on the mountain and the whole thing was under about 400 inches of snow. You could launch off anything and land in these huge pillows of fresh powder, it was like a playground out there and all the lines in the trees were deep and fresh just about every other day. We knew we needed to take that board through the trees on a whiteout day so that there was no chance to be seen by patrol or any tourists lost in the woods. Even though Perkins had sacrificed the thing over the grease pit, he claimed to love it, but for all the wrong reasons, you know? He loved it like a museum piece and Sweeney and I knew Brosnan never made a board in his life that wasn't meant to be ridden in big surf.

"The thing is, and it's really sad, Brosnan kind of dropped out of surfing in the early '6os as Hawaii was getting mobbed. He went to Peru for a while, I think, and then when he heard that the World Championships were gonna be down there he just disappeared. No one really heard from him for years. I've read a couple articles about the guy and Sweeney told me all about him, too. Brosnan was supposed to be in South Africa and then in Ireland, but he really was tough to track down. The FBI was looking for him because of some embezzlement charge or something, but no one could find him. Brosnan was from the old school of surfing. He used to drink and surf and brawl with the locals, the Hawaiians, after every big day at Waimea. The locals loved him over there because he was a lot like them, just smaller.

When he traveled he kinda stopped shaping boards, but then after he got out of jail he was down in Baja making foam guns and drinking a ton. They say he died after about a year or two down there. Died from drinking too much. Those few foam boards, like the one over that fryolater, showed that Brosnan still had the touch—even if he was drinking up the profits from each board.

"Sorry, I went off on a tangent there. Even now, I remember how much Sweeney loved that surfboard in the lodge. It was as close to Ronnie Brosnan as he was gonna get in his lifetime. And he told me most of the stuff I know about Brosnan, I'm just passing it on to you. The only reason I didn't pull the thing down when I first saw it was because Perkins had the decency to hang the thing with fishing line—rather than driving screws through it. Thank God. If he had impaled the thing I'd be in Pelican Bay doing time for manslaughter.

"Oh yeah, so the plan goes like this: Sweeney and me only let one other guy in on it—this ski patroller, Jan (pronounced Yahn). Jan had surfed a little, admitted that he sucked at it, but he said he knew a good board when he saw it. I knew he'd be cool with helping us. Jan Solo, which is what the staff on the mountain called him, was this huge, almost stereotypical Swedish-American guy. He had the huge reddish-blonde beard, the hulking frame, big smile, happiest when it was below zero and blowing for days. You know the type of guy. He was even from Minnesota! No shit. From some little town up north— Longville, I think. He got Sweeney a job doing tree work up there one spring or summer—it's up by the Boundary Waters near the Canadian Border. Jan was a great guy, and he helped us out a ton because he agreed to let me and Sweeney use his patrol sled for 60 minutes. No more than that, because if some gaper wrapped himself around a tree in that time—and a sled was missing—then it was back to freezing, flat Minnesota for his Swedish ass. I think Jan Solo, instinctively, didn't understand a guy like Gene Perkins, so he was game for our gun heist.

"Me and Sweeney met up at the lodge at exactly 12:15 p.m. on a Saturday of the Xmas-New Year's vacation week. It was nearly whiteout conditions—about 20 or 25 degrees with a storm dumping big wet flakes all day long. But the lodge was still pretty crowded because it was one of the peak weekends of the year. We hoped for a little chaos when it all went down, so we were in good shape. We'd stashed a big rusty pair of hedge clippers in the snow out by the side exit of the lodge, nearest to the Brosnan, and marked it with a pair of ski poles. Jan Solo had skied the clippers to the lodge at about ten to noon and I met him near the back of the lodge and pulled the clippers out from under the blankets on his patrol sled. He then left the sled down by the same side exit. The patrol guys sometimes left sleds there around lunchtime, so it didn't look out of place.

"Me and Sweeney went inside and got in line at 'The Kahuna Grille' while Jan Solo made himself scarce. We didn't need him for anything else until he was gonna meet us above the patrol shack, and he didn't want to be connected any further than the placement and pick-up of the sled. I had a citronella candle in my pocket and Sweeney stood a few people behind me in line. We'd changed out of our resort jackets and kept our hats on and our goggles around our necks. The line was really long, so we waited until we were about 8 or 10 people away from the front of the line. Then Sweeney signaled to me and I went back into the bathroom and lit the candle beneath the smoke alarm in the bathroom. It was the old fire-alarm trick. It had gotten us out of many an exam at Seawell High School and Sweeney felt it wouldn't let us down.

"So I came back out and give him a nod as he starts to order a 'Santa Fe chicken burrito, please. Hold the guacamole, beans, onions, salsa, cheese, and I guess I better not eat any sour cream either.'

The kid looks at Sweeney and goes, 'So...you want just chicken in the tortilla?'

Sweeney says, 'Yeah, I guess. You think that's weird? I don't think it's any weirder than eating a fake Mexican burrito from a poser-Hawaiian fast food place in an imitation Bavarian ski lodge while enjoying turns in the deep powder of western North America.' Sweeney had figured out that a little geography and a few cultural references tacked onto any comment made most teenage ski bums' heads spin.

The kid looks up at Sweeney like some sort of wounded primate and goes, 'Dude, what's wrong with you? You like laptose intolerant or something?' Apparently the geography and cultural comparisons didn't even register with that jackass. He heard Sweeney's order and then, 'Blah, blah, blah....' I heard Sweeney say, 'Yeah, that's right, Julia Child, so just give me the Santa Fe burrito with the chicken and maybe a little cheese. You happy?'

"Then, in the middle of what I imagined was his response of, 'Whatever, dude,' the fire alarm goes off—way louder than I expected. Me and Sweeney throw our trays and silverware back over our heads and scream like 12-year-old girls at a horror flick, and the whole place goes fuckin' crazy. Just...fuckin'...bananas! It was hilarious. We both pulled on our goggles and zipped up our jackets over our mouths. I ran over to the side exit and squeezed through the throng of people pushing their way through the door. I held it open for everyone and pretended to shepherd the gapers out into the safety of the blizzard conditions, yelling, 'Jesus, people, save the skis! For the love of Christ, think of the skis!'

"Sweeney went directly to the bathroom and grabbed the candle and shoved it in his pocket. He came out the exit in the middle of a crowd and he pretended to trip and shoved me and like five gapers into the snowbank. Everyone screamed, the door banged into some spacey kid's head, and everyone rolled around in the snow while I dug out the clippers—trying not to laugh and throwing a few uncalled-for elbows.

"Gracefully executed? No. Effective? Pretty much.

"So everyone basically got out the door and they were all trying to collect their skis and snowboards and poles and shit out of all the racks next to the building. People were dropping mittens and zipping up their one-piece Bogners and the whole scene was a joke. Everyone's so concerned with their gear that me and Sweeney prop open the door with the patrol sled from the other side of the snowbank without anyone even watching us. It was all working smoothly. At this point, we heard the ski patrol clomping through the front door of the lodge, upstairs, so we knew we only had a little time. Sweeney and me run in back to the fryolater, and I reach up and clip the fishing line, one and two, and the Brosnan slipped into Sweeney's waiting arms. It was that simple. The feeling of those rails in Sweeney's hands was just shinin' through his ear-to-ear grin. He knew he had a Brosnan and knew he would ride it in the sort of waves it was made for.

"Next thing we did was I went back to the sled that was holding the door open. By then, a few people were kind of looking our way, though they couldn't see too much through the snow. I'm yelling out the door, in my best junior-high, high-pitched voice, 'No worries, gapers, nothing to see here. Just a small grease fire, everything's under the bowl, we'll have this cable up in time for your soaps, snow berries. . .' and so on and so forth. I'm just spitting out nonsense and nobody can hear me over the alarm and the wind and snow anyway. It was like herding sheep in a hurricane—just chaos.

"So then I grabbed an extra blanket that Jan Solo left on the sled for the purpose and I made like I was gonna run in and smother the fire. Sweeney wrapped up the bottom half of the board in the blanket. I ran back to the sled and grabbed the other blanket, unfolded it and held it in front of the door with my arms over his head. As soon as I block everyone's view, Sweeney runs over and slides the half-wrapped board into the sled. I drop the blanket in my hands on the board. We gently strap it into the sled and pull it out from the door. A couple people asked us what was going on in there. Sweeney babbled something about a panic attack, a hairnet and the fryolater, and we kept moving, dragging the sled around the corner behind us. No one asked what was in the sled because it looked pretty flat and empty with just the board under the blankets.

"The Brosnan's single, semi-transparent, red, fiberglass fin stuck out of the blankets at the bottom of the sled and I prayed that no one saw it, and I'm pretty sure no one did. I clicked into my waiting skis, strapped on the sled and took off toward the nearest trees. Sweeney jumped into his snowboard bindings and followed. He told me that the red fin cut through the powder like the fin from some sort of snow-shark.

"Jan Solo had given me a quick lesson on how to ski with a sled behind me, and I had done some patrolling for like a month back East at Nashoba Valley so I was doing okay with the thing. Sweeney caught up to me in the trees and he was laughing his ass off and imitating my tray-throwing scream from when the fire alarm went off, and he could scream pretty damn well himself. We laughed for a minute or two, and then we calmed ourselves and made our way through the trees, across the mountain and out of bounds. We hiked up a little bit to the snow cave we had constructed for the purpose of storing the board for a few days. Sweeney had plastered the inner walls of the shrine with pictures of firing Honolua Bay, 30-foot Waimea closeout sets, and shots of Brosnan with his balsa boards back in the '50s. It was like a little frozen slice of Hawaii in there, couple pineapples stuck in the snow and stuff like that. I'd even constructed a little altar for the board to rest on, with two chairs dug out of the walls so that we could stare at the board and drink a couple cans of beer to celebrate the resurrection of the Brosnan. But, by the time we got to the cave, the 60-minute limit on the patrol sled rental was up. We shotgunned our beers, said goodbye to the gun, and I brought the sled back to a mogul run above the patrol shack where Jan Solo took it over and brought it home. Jan Solo was all smiles when he heard the board was safely in the cave. He said he'd meet us there at nine, well after the mountain closed, to check out the board and have a few beers.

"Me, Sweeney and Jan Solo met that night and we each drank a six pack and sat by the Brosnan and admired it in the lantern light on its altar of snow: Three grown men, in silence, staring at a real Ronnie Brosnan. Jan Solo wasn't really even a surfer, but he hung out for a long time—the board was that pretty. Three days later, we met again at nine p.m. and gently strapped the board onto another patrol sled and skied the thing down to my car, which was waiting in the backcountry shuttle parking lot out by the road through the pass.

"Within a month, Sweeney had gotten the Brosnan down

to Black's Beach in San Diego. I gave him a week or two off. He told me he caught a day with 12- to 15-foot faces, offshore Santa Ana winds and a good sized crowd of people out there with him.

"Lookit, I can't really explain the elation he must've felt when he paddled out on that board. Some of it was still showing in his eyes when he told me about it a week later. It would be impossible for me to describe how it slid down the face of that first greenish A-frame, but I can imagine. Well, I guess I can imagine because I started going to Hawaii myself in the summers after that winter. I decided I wanted to learn how to surf after helping to liberate the Brosnan. When I think back on that winter, though, I still like to imagine how it must have felt for Sweeney on that first day at Blacks—how he must've felt on the fade to the left and the first bottom turn up under the lip; how the sunlight filtered down onto the droplets dancing near the red, shining nose of that board. I can see him setting the rail on the wave's face, looking up and out toward the light as the whole wave bowled around him. I can feel how fast that board cruised out of the shade of that barrel with ease.

"He described it to me more than once, 'I just let it do its thing, man. I wish you were there to see it come out of that barrel—the closest I've ever been to a state of grace.'

"I heard a rumor that Sweeney had someone send a photo of him in that barrel to Gene Perkins a couple months later. I don't know about that, but I've always held out hope that he did."

LOUD
The quick chirp of a disarmed car alarm
wakens me to the rustling at three thousand
meters: the creaks and murmurs in the building;
the thud of un fútbol in a courtyard;
cabs honk as they bump toward each intersection;
the "*Buenos Días*" of the indigenous
beneath the heft of baskets that are bound
to their backs, held close, with blankets grey and taut.

SOFT
They've walked down from Pichinchas broad, green steeps,
speckled and veined with blue and whitewashed homes.
And los nublados slip along the ridge,
the low clouds push and pull like bent, licked paws
along the verdant flanks of the volcano.

SUSTAIN
In the afternoon, the rain spatters the bricks,
sunwarmed cobblestone sidewalks, wrinkled asphalt;
the flat, wet smell of the pavement commingles
with the coaldark rank of combusted gas.
And the cops will whistle, as clouds thicken and wisp
above thin men on mopeds, as the Quichua
lead travellers with a trail of fresh scent
drifting from their bushels of flowers and herbs—
the scent grafted to my limbs, an echo becoming
the cradled blooms of my frail, seedling poems.

—Sweeney

(Postmarked in Ecuador, 1997.)

Chapter 8

THE "DOCTAH" AND THE CURSE

I'd been unable to find out much about Sweeney's life in the few months leading up to his original stint in The Merritt House of Corrections. Then I heard that Sweeney's cousin, Tommy—a local at McSwiggans—was good for a couple of Sweeney stories after he'd had a few. I went and found him on a Tuesday night at McSwiggans and bought him several pints.

Tommy's a big guy—he says he's "pushin' three bills these days" and he has a thick, brown goatee hanging off his face. He's worked at "Duck Island," Seawell's sewage-treatment plant, since shortly after he graduated from high school.

Other than cutting out a few of Tommy's tangents about Sweeney's penchant for bedhead and why "The Doctah,"aka Doctor MacGillicuddy's, a brand of peppermint Schnaaps, is so popular in Seawell, I have transcribed his story word for word. I asked Tommy to tell me about what happened to Sweeney the summer before he went to Merritt for fifteen months. The following interview was from my first meeting with Tommy Santos.

It's funny I'm tellin' you this, 'cuz just the other day I was sayin' to Spiro, that's Billy Spiroulakis, that I couldn't figure out for the life of me what the hell two Mormons were thinking when they went out to Farannan to try and "save" Sweeney's soul. I mean, what the fuck were they thinkin'?

Sweeney was drinking heavy back then—this was when he was around nineteen or twenty, I guess. He was drinking even more than usual 'cuz there hadn't been waves in a couple months. He'd been down in Mexico all spring—this was just after he'd fucked up the whole Pepperdine thing in the middle of '89. In like, March, I think, he disappeared down to Baja, and then came back to Seawell just in time to miss the cuts for [The Seawell City Golf Tournament]. He was in rough shape, there was some weird shit going on with him and his family and girlfriend back then. And those poor Mormon kids just picked the wrong time, just the fucking worst time, to try and talk to Sweeney.

Sweeney was tellin' Goatboy about the whole thing, like the night after it happened. Sweeney wasn't really talkin' to me back then; we had a falling out over some family shit earlier that summer. But I still hung out with him, with that same crew, you know what I mean?

A big group of us were playing cards at The South End Club, early, and Sweeney'd been in this weird mood, laughing to himself the whole time. Some guys asked him what he was laughing about, and to shut the hell up, "We're playing 45s not fuckin' double-dutch," and stuff like that, just givin' him shit. Sweeney said he wasn't gonna tell anybody about it but then he was, like, "This is too funny *not* to tell you guys." So he finally went into the whole thing after him and Goatboy lost to a pair of 75-year-old Polish women who played 45s like a couple professionals. Those Polish old maids take that shit seriously—they do *not* fuck around.

But, regardless, we finished up the tournament and a bunch of us went over to The Wardin so he could tell the story. We got some beers and all went upstairs, there were about eight or nine of us—me, Goatboy; Smitty, the Spiroulakis brothers, Dennis Laverty; Tweedy and Speck, and a maybe a couple other people.

Sweeney starts by tellin' us he was all hungover the morning these Mormon kids showed up at his door. He was trying to sleep it off, but the groundskeeping shed was getting hot in the sun. Back then, he used to stay in the groundskeeper's shed in the woods off number six on Farannan Golf Course when he was too drunk to walk the 200 yards past the garage in the woods. He had an old boat, a big old trawler, up on barrels out in the woods, he lived in the thing so he could be close to the surf spot right near there, but he kept falling in the ditch back there when he was drunk and he'd wake up all hungover and smellin' like skunk weed. But, anyways, Sweeney tells us he hears this knock on the door of the garage the other morning. He's like, "Who the fuck would be knocking on the door?" His head was killin' him and he doesn't want to answer the door because he's sure it's just Mick with the garden hose ready to soak his sorry ass. But he hears these mumbles and more knocking. Then he hears a squeaky voice say, "It's Elder so-and-so and Brother what's-his-face," or whateverthefuck they call themselves.

Sweeney just gets annoyed. He said he was psyched that he woke up and he didn't smell like skunk weed, but he's still fuckin' hungover and somehow these little tie-wearin' bastards had walked all the way out on the course to try and talk to him. He had no idea how the fuck they knew he was there. He said he thought it was kind of weird at the time, but he's sort of impressed that they found him, so as he's layin' there he decides to just laugh it off and have some fun with the kids. Harmless shit, ya know?

He wraps his blanket around him and jumps up and sneaks to the garage door. He unlocks the thing quietly, trying to hold onto the blanket. And then, while the kids are still knocking on the storm door to the left of the garage, he throws up the garage door as hard as he fuckin' can—trying to scare the hell outta the kids. But, when Sweeney throws up the door—and I was just describin' this moment to my cousin down in Lynn the other day—a nail or bolt or somethin' caught the Mexican blanket and just ripped it clean off of him. So there he is, naked as a jaybird, showin' a rabid case of bedhead, with a couple of virgin Mormon kids going pale and falling all over each other tryin' to get away from the sight of it.

Sweeney decides he better keep going with the joke, before he breaks down laughing, so he starts yelling about how, "Jesus can go to hell and Joseph the Prophet can suck a dick!" And, "Who the fuck dares knock at this ungodly hour of 9:35..." And he's waving his arms and jumping up and down and trying to look crazy, an' shit like that. Sweeney told us he started doing the Chicken Dance in the driveway while he was yelling all the blasphemous shit he could think of. He said he was trying to keep from laughing out loud at the sight of the Mormons' faces, and somehow doing the Chicken distracted him from how funny the whole thing was. I kinda understand, 'cuz I get depressed every time I see people doin' the Chicken at a wedding or a Jack 'n' Jill. It's fuckin' degradin' to see a guy, drunk as hell, flappin' his elbows an' shit. I fuckin' hate it.

On the other hand, picturin' Sweeney doin' the Chicken buck-naked kinda sucks, too. I mean, we all loved the guy, but he was fuckin' haunted a little bit, ya know? But he told a good story, so we were all listenin' to every word outta his mouth that night.

Anyways, Sweeney was dyin' laughin at The Wardin while he was telling us about how the kids were backing away and tripping over tree roots and how their jaws dropped. They were just fuckin' horrified. I wished I'd been there to see it, it musta been a riot.

See, some of us kinda knew Sweeney didn't really like organized religion, most of us were raised Catholic and he would give us shit, but I never heard him say anything bad to a stranger or insult somebody he didn't know—like insult their beliefs or anything. Sweeney just worked on his own level, he left people alone unless someone tried to tell him what to think or believe. That's the only time I ever saw him get pissed and rant about religion.

And the thing is, I knew he was a smart bastard but he never came across that way. He had all these piles of books about Buddhism and tons of stuff by Steinbeck. He could speak Spanish and stuff. I remember when we were teenagers he read *War and Peace* and fuckin' *Roots* in one summer. He was fuckin' nuts! He always had tons of books lying around the garage and out on his boat in the woods, lots of poetry too. Not many other people knew how smart he was. He was just like all the other guys when we were hanging out drinkin' an' shit. It's just that he was way smarter than all of us, and a better athlete, and he could've kicked all our asses at once—well, maybe not at once, but you know what I'm sayin'. He was just better at everything without even trying.

The thing is, back then, when we were all in our early twenties or so, he didn't have any sort of outlet other than traveling. At least, that's my theory now that I've thought about it. The traveling thing seemed to work for him. Before he started traveling regularly, before he went to prison, like around the time these Mormon kids tried to save him, he just got hammered a lot. He never drank when there were waves, but the summer flat spells would drive him down to The Wardin or over to The Harbor

Court's upstairs deck like four or five nights a week.

So, anyways, sorry, I got off track there. As far as those Mormon kids go, Sweeney told us he was just trying to have fun with them when he tried to scare them. He didn't like some 17-year-old asking him "Do you ever feel lost?" but he felt sorry for the brainwashed fuckers so he didn't want to hurt them, really. But that day he scared those two kids so bad they fell in the mud and got their white shirts all dirty, and then they ran across Farannan and back to their cheap mountain bikes. When they turned around to run, I guess one of 'em dropped his Bible. Sweeney chased after them for like a hundred yards waving the book around, and then he threw it into the pond near the tee on number nine. One of the kids actually stopped when he saw him throw it, and yelled back something like, You're cursed, you madman, Yardbird Sweeney! You can't get away with that! And only God may save you! or some kinda bullshit.

Sweeney said he was a little weirded-out by the kid knowing his name, but since it was only the old timers at the course who called him "Yardbird" he figured it was one of them that sent the kids out to the groundskeeping shed as a joke in the first place.

Other than telling us the story in the bar that night, and laughin' until he was cryin'—we were all laughin' pretty hard that night—Sweeney didn't seem to think too much about the whole thing. He didn't really talk about it much. I mean, that summer, you could get Sweeney to imitate his naked Chicken Dance after he'd had a few, but that was about it would go. And these days, if I go to tell the story, turns out not many people have heard it before.

Even though *he* didn't talk about it much, to be honest, and I've thought about this a lot, I think things did kind of go to hell for Sweeney after that. A little while after that, Goatboy had to tell him he couldn't stay out on his boat or in the groundskeeping shed for a while because some golfers complained to the pro. So he lost his places to stay near his favorite surf spots, and then there wasn't much tree work for him to do that month either, and there were no waves. It was one of the worst summers for waves in a long time in Seawell, I remember people complainin' in the bars. The Atlantic looked like a freakin' lake. Sweeney had been down in Baja a little before that, just surfing his balls off all spring. I think it was like two months later, during that flat spell, sometime in August or something, when he got in that brawl in North Seawell.

Has anyone told you about that? I mean, I'm sure you heard he went to Merritt for fighting and stuff, but have you heard about the actual fight? No? Well, get another Car Bomb set up.

Hey, Jamesayyy! Set us both up with Irish Car Bombs, on my tab!

I'm gonna go take a piss and then I'll tell you all about it. This is a crazy fuckin' story!

Okay, let me down this thing and then we're on [*gulps down a shot of Jamesons whiskey dropped in half a pint of Guinness*]. Okay, like I said, Sweeney was drinking like every other night down at The Wardin that summer. After the Mormon incident, he kinda snapped. He didn't have any patience with anyone he didn't know. I mean, he was cool with all of us, but that was 'cuz we drank with him and had gone to high school an' shit with him. We loved the guy, he was sort of like a hero to most of us for all the shit I've been telling you about. But that month he was starting fights, rather than trying to calm things down and only fighting if he had to. He was actin' different. I think it was because of the Mormons, but also because he owed Pedro [his bookie] like a grand. He finally had to pay up on that ridiculous bet on the B.C. Eagles during March Madness the year before—fuckin' idiot. Everyone told him not to make that bet, but he did it anyway—stubborn prick. So, he ended up putting off traveling for a few months and I think that got to him. He started spending the money he had on Guinness and The Doctah—just drinkin' like a fish.

He'd been fighting all these guys from Galloway and Lawrence during that month. It was fun for him. He'd get piss-drunk and start something with whoever else looked like they wanted to fight. He'd broke one guy's nose for playing some New

Kids on the Block song on the jukebox at The Blue Limerick, or something like that. Guys were steerin' clear of him by then.

Then, on a Saturday night near the end of the summer, these guys from Galloway brought like a dozen friends into Seawell to find him. He was drinking up near the beach in North Seawell, in Sun Valley, because that's where all the summer people go and rent houses and party and shit. It's fun there in the summer. A couple of us were with him at this place on Maghrath St., but it wasn't our regular place. We liked the bars downtown. So, anyways, these Galloway guys come in and Sweeney's actin' like he's got a death wish or something. He's ordering pints of Guinness and chuckin' 'em at these guys—I know! Alcohol abuse, right! He's just wastin' beer, throwin' it at people whenever the bartender isn't looking, throwin' his cigarettes and lighter an' shit. It's fuckin' nuts. Like four of the Galloway guys jump up and one huge guy holds 'em all back, and just before the bartender tosses all of us—and this was fuckin' perfect—the music stops and Sweeney gets off his stool, looks the huge guy up and down and says, "If you're feelin' froggy…then leap, suckah!"

And that guy started to leap, he was keyed-up, but we all stopped it and brought it outside.

So we all go outside, and it's like twelve of them on seven or eight of us, but Sweeney was in rare form. He was just dropping people left and right with elbows and uppercuts and wrestling take-downs. He could box a little bit and he could wrestle an' shit. He was goin' off. It was fucking nuts.

It got to the point where the Galloway guys sort of stopped comin' after us and we sort of stopped goin' after them, and we were all just watching Sweeney finish off the huge guy he talked shit to inside the bar. The guy was way bigger than Sweeney. The guy was a fuckin' monster. But Sweeney could fight. He wrestled one-sixty-threes or something when he was a sophomore, I forget what weight, but he was smart and fast. He got up close and quick on this guy and had his mouth all bloody, and then ankle-picked him and the guy went flying back. Before he even landed Sweeney was on top of him, with one of his legs locked up, just pounding him in the face. They rolled off the sidewalk, it's like a raised sidewalk outside that bar, and the guy's head hit the cement or somethin', 'cuz he was sort of knocked out for a second. Sweeney got up and was yelling at the guy to get up, and we were tellin' Sweeney to calm down 'cuz it was obvious to everyone there the fight was over.

This part's fucked up, just fucked. Because, as I'm grabbing Sweeney's right arm, but before I really got ahold of him, one of those two Mormon kids came up behind us—the same little fuckers from the golf course. They came outta nowhere, the stupid little shits. I think it was the one who'd lost his Bible in the pond. I guess the Mormon kids were living somewhere nearby in North Seawell, out by the marsh I guess. Not the nicest part of town, but that's where they had their apartment. So Elder what's-his-face comes up behind us just as I'm trying to grab Sweeney. He gets his hand on Sweeney's left arm and starts to say something. Sweeney turns around, like, frothing at the mouth, and just lays the poor kid out with a left-handed haymaker. It was fucked.

He sort of lost it right there—personally, I think that's when Sweeney hit bottom. He was all flighty, his eyes were rollin' around in his head. He musta been out of his mind, because he usually fought fair if he fought at all. The poor Elder-kid's jaw was shattered by that one punch. I saw his eyes go blank, and his face got limp and pale while he was falling to the street. It was, like, in slow-mo, ya know what I mean? It was fuckin' crazy. He slipped off the sidewalk, landed in an oily puddle and his head cracked a parking block. It was disgusting—his face was a mess, and it was probably better that he was knocked out cold.

About five or six of us jumped on Sweeney and held him down and kept the Galloway guys away from him. We're all bleeding on each other and Sweeney's just freaking out beneath us. The Galloway guys were kinda picking up their own guy, the monster, and then they were just staring at all of us and Sweeney. And just then the other Mormon kid comes up and he's jumping around in his white shirt and tie and he's freaking out about his friend's face. So, Laverty's trying to hold that kid back from moving his friend around and the kid's yelling that he's already called the cops and telling Sweeney he's going to hell and all that shit. I can see Laverty wants to slap the kid, in spite of himself. I'm tellin' him to calm down. Meanwhile, there's blood dripping out of the other Mormon's ears, and it's takin' the rest of us, like six of us, to hold Sweeney down because he was still fuckin' acting like an animal. The Galloway guys stuffed their monster in the back of a Jetta and took off, and then about four cop cars pull up and see the poor Mormon kid laid out in the puddle. They pepper-spray Sweeney, cuff him and throw him in the paddy wagon in about five seconds flat. No questions asked.

We were on Sweeney's side, but we couldn't believe that he'd just knocked that kid out. And, for once, I didn't really recognize any of the cops. A couple of us—Laverty was one of 'em— thought Sweeney didn't know who he hit. Some of us thought he did. I still don't know. And the cops were everywhere before we could think straight. I'd had too much of the Doctah' that night, and my eyes were pretty much swelling shut by that point. I was just stunned by the whole thing. We should of let Sweeney take off, the cops never would've caught him, the guy knew how to disappear quick. But we were all kinda freaked by the sight of the unconscious kid on the ground; Spiro was screaming for someone to call an ambulance; the other Mormon's still jumping around yellin' all kinds of fire-and-brimstone type shit. It wasn't pretty and never got any prettier.

I remember watchin' the paddy wagon pull away, and thinkin' that Sweeney might need to do some time to calm down a little. What was it with his record? Like, 18 months at Merritt? I don't know, I forget. But I realize now that it wasn't any good for him. It didn't do him any fuckin' good at all.

Because when Sweeney got out, we didn't really hang out much after that. I didn't see him at The Wardin or even McSwiggans anymore, and I was there a lot. I mean, he was still pissed at me for the stuff in Mexico that past June, but it wasn't that bad between us. We were patchin' things up slowly. But Sweeney just kind of faded in and out for a few years after that. Everyone was telling us he was living over on the golf course again, in his old boat, the Kemp Aaberg—which, he was. . .sometimes. But then I'd hear he was in Mexico, and then Ireland. I heard crazy, erratic shit. Then I started hearin' Sweeney went fuckin' bananas while he was in Merritt and that the government was giving him money to live on.

I don't know. I didn't know what to do about the guy.

I didn't really know what was true or what, even though I'm his cousin. I mean, what was I supposed to do? Go over to the golf course and start looking in the out-of-bounds areas for him—up in the trees an' shit? He was still kinda pissed at me, and I couldn't blame the guy. But I was still kinda pissed he stopped playin' baseball and that he quit school. So I wouldn't-ah-known what to say if I found him out in the forest or some-where. I mean, every once in a while, we'd gone over and hung out with him on his boat in the woods, but I was engaged back then and I was catchin' hell for goin' out and getting shitfaced and all that. I wasn't seeing too much of him or any of the other guys at the time.

I remember bein' like, "Fuck it, he knows how to take care of himself." I just let it all go.

You know what I mean? Sweeney was always the type of guy who would just show up and hang out and drink an' shit. You never called him, he'd always just be there on the best nights an' stuff. He knew everything that was going on, I just sort of fol-lowed his lead back then. I didn't know how to help someone like that.

I think about it now, sometimes, and I guess *anything* would've been better than nothing. I shoulda come clean with the guy.

I mean, well, this is all I'll say: at this point—and I think about this a lot, Owen—I just wish I'd tried something, that I'd done something different. You know what I mean?

FRANCISCO "PANCHO" MONEYMAKER

Once told me, "I only hear
Dixieland, no matter what
comes my way." He always rode
his piebald mare with a flat,
broad machete hung from his
left hand, rope-reins in his right.
He bobbed to the rise and fall
of the mare's slow clop, danced
through muddy, rock-strewn streambeds.
His machete thwacked through vines
and green jungled undergrowth
like a rusty metronome.
He built a small farm, and grew
passion fruits, corn, peanuts and weed.
The chickens were happy there—
plump from smoke-induced feeding
frenzies Pancho blew into
their flock.　　　When he needed cash
Pancho dug ditches in town:
"It's honest work, if you can
sweat it," he grinned. "Dirt-road towns
need ditches. It's straightforward
here; when it's shallow they say,
'*superficial*,' and my
sweat makes it '*más profundo.*'"

—Sweeney

"THE SEED," PANCHO'S DREAM
Late Saturday night, Pancho spoke the dream.
He chanted its deep swerve and benthic sway.
I listened, seated, leaning against salt-bleached
driftwood logs, sifting sand through my cupped hands.
Three days before, we'd crushed the skull of a quarter
horse, a spooked, brownish mare that lurched from the ditch
grasses to the right of our borrowed Toyota.
Pancho's head hung over the tiny peaks
of sand burying his tanned, calloused feet.
The firelight licked at the crown of his head
as words crept through the veil of his long hair:

Neon vines sprout in my virgin jungle, low
in the ferns, their unraveled reds split hues of green
evening as dusk unfolds. And dusk spreads slow

as rust clotting the gears of an old machine.
When darkness floods, suddenly, it's a spate
of hungry bats blackening the skies of the scene.

I feel the Earth pulse, like a fuse blown straight
out of its box. It teeters in search of its lost
thread: the long orbit plotted by its own weight.

In a flash, my jungle goes cold. A dense hoarfrost
seizes the undergrowth and shorts the neon.
Bright vines explode, sparks shower, thrown and tossed

by freezing winds. I wilt beneath the strewn
sparks, their wide glare reddening the frosts' white spread.
Blown-glass clouds gather, backed by a dark, moon-

less night—their blue-black underbellies touched
with white reflections of the rime that chokes
the web of jungle life. Soon, it will be dead.

I move slow—cold, static—but my body soaks
my clothes with sweat. White-hot secrets stab down
from clouds in the tilted sky. The thigh-thick spokes

of lightning chisel the icy ground and stun
me into a world gone black and white. Each moment
conducts the next, but connects with the mare's last one:

when her round eye fogged like some animate,
rolling sky blotted with shock. But then the dream
shifts as the clouds thin, break and dissipate.

The sun rages, though light rain pelts low steam
that's slung around the brown trunks of thin trees.
The trunks resemble limbs jutting from a stream

of stretched gauze. But the truth tugs me to my knees,
struck dumb, staring at a field of birth-wet foals
sown hoof-deep. The Earth's brood incubated by breeze

and sunshower—I'm entranced till something rolls
in my palm. The vision blurs, and I understand
her eye's a seed in my care. My whole arm tolls

in time with the throb of that surging ground.
There is no knell in the pulse of the green world.
And I slip from that potent fountainhead

electric and awake; back to the sound
of my farm in the heart of the jungle—where trees seem to graze
on silence budding between footfalls of wind.

Pancho paused, stared at our fire, his yellowed gaze
subdued, and said one more thing before he left:
"I read once that at any given moment
one hundred bolts of lightning strike the Earth,
each sheathed in a column of thunder. We survive…
we grope along on pulmonary ground—
between the beats and breaths of this green fuse."

—Sweeney, as told to me by Francisco Moneymaker.

(Both of these poems take place somewhere in Central or South America.
Yet, each arrived separately, within the same month from Galway, Ireland,
in 1997. Both were written in green ink on paper designed to fold up into
its own air-mail envelope.)

CHAPTER 9

THE BLOWN FREE RIDE

*The following is an interview with Audrey Gammens. Audrey has
written and edited for Seawell's newspaper,* The Seawell Times*, for
twenty-five years. She originally covered the local sports scene—
Seawell State University, Seawell High School, and the Red Sox single-A affiliate, the Seawell Gulls. Eventually, Audrey began covering
the Sox down in Boston, often travelling to Fenway for important
games, post-game interviews and general coverage of the club.
Audrey left* The Seawell Times *for several years and freelanced as a
writer and editor. Many of her articles appeared in* The Boston
Herald*,* The Boston Globe *and occasionally in* The Sporting News
*as well as other national sports publications. Baseball has always
been her "beat," and Audrey was one of the first female sportswrit-
ers to be accepted into the old-boys media-coverage scene in the
Boston area.*

*Born and raised just outside of Seawell in Galloway,
Audrey eventually returned to* The Seawell Times *to woman the
helm as Sports Editor.*

*Ms. Gammens, thanks for agreeing to this interview, I know you are
very busy at the paper and you don't have much time.*
Not a problem. Please, call me Audrey and forgive me if this is a
little awkward. I'll have to get used to being the interviewee. I'm
usually on the other side of the tape recorder.

*Not a problem, Audrey, I'm sure you'll do fine. Please feel free to
help me out with my lack of skill as an interviewer. This project has
forced me to appreciate the art of asking the right questions, but I've
still got a lot to learn.*

*I just wanted to ask you about your days covering Seawell
High baseball, back when Yardbird Sweeney was playing shortstop
for the varsity team as a sophomore.*
Oh, well you're doing fine, just fine so far. You're asking about a
very specific period of time, and I remember Sweeney very well.
He was one of the best players Seawell High has ever seen. He
was their shortstop, but over those four years I saw him try his
hand at catcher, outfielder and almost every other position in the
field. He was nearly a complete player, which is very rare at that

age. The coach back then, Jorge Mroz, had a pretty good eye for talent and he worked Sweeney into his lineup every chance he could during Sweeney's freshman and sophomore years. I believe Coach Mroz would've made Sweeney a starter at short as a sophomore, but there's a heavy amount of politics to be negotiated within the coaching of Seawell's varsity squads. As a junior, however, Sweeney had earned the spot at short, occasionally backing up as catcher when needed. Those were Sweeney's two best positions, defensively. Which, if you know baseball, you know it's odd for a player to be able to grind out a game behind the plate one day and then have the range and quickness to play the next game at shortstop.

Could you elaborate a little on that. I'm not really up to speed on the finer points of baseball.
Certainly, I'd be happy to. You see, Sweeney, back then, was around five-foot-ten or so. He wasn't thin but he wasn't stocky like your average catcher, either. He was an athlete, around one-hundred and sixty or seventy pounds. He was lanky or even lithe. Yes, "lithe" would be an accurate word to describe him. I believe he ran the 110 hurdles during the winter as well. I remember that he physically looked more the part of a shortstop, but once he threw on the equipment he was every bit of a catcher as well. He had a cannon for an arm, so there was no problem there—he could throw a runner out at second from his knees, but he could also turn a double play as if he were never hurried to make the play. I would equate him, now, to Montreal's Orlando Cabrera, a guy who has fun playing short every day and does it with ease. When he caught, Sweeney always reminded me of Pudge Fisk, the old Sox catcher. Sweeney had that same nonchalance as Pudge, and that quality is rare in a catcher.

       I remember distinctly, and you might find this in some of my old columns about those high school teams, that he was a natural. He could hit any pitch from either side of the plate, lay down a drag bunt with the best of lefties, he had some power from the left side and his swing was smooth and even. Overall, very pretty to watch when he was up at the plate.

As for the defensive end of things, he really could've played anywhere on that field—as I've said before. Seawell always had strong pitching in those days, so he wasn't needed there, to my recollection. But I seem to recall that he gave every other position a go—and he handled it all smoothly. Struggle was not a part of his game. He seemed to glide through every play I saw him make. Most importantly, and this is the aspect of his game I most enjoyed, he always looked like he was having fun out there. He was, at least until his senior year, constantly smiling and laughing—constantly at play, as a high school player should be.

So, Sweeney was a different sort of player as a senior?
Well, I recall that he seemed to lose touch with how much fun he was having out there. It was only a few games into his senior year and I noticed how he had lost that verve, and he was playing with a little more aggression, a little more anger. At least, it appeared that way to me. As a fan, I was disappointed to see this subtle change in his game. Although, I recall that his numbers weren't affected. He still hit cleanup and was All-State, and his defense never suffered. He never revealed to me the cause of this change. I never pushed the issue in the few brief interviews I did with him that year. I wanted to, desperately, but I kept reminding myself that he was just a kid playing baseball. He wore his heart on his sleeve, that was clear, but he was just an extremely talented kid, and it didn't seem fair of me to delve into anything in his personal life that might have affected his game. Really, as I've said, it was a subtle change in his playing style that not too many people noticed. I suppose I only noticed because I'd seen him grow into a star in the Seawell High program. Baseball is my first love, and he was a player I'd spent a lot of time watching.

Could you speculate as to what might have caused the change?
Well, yes, I suppose I could. I once spoke with Jorge Mroz about it because, as I've said, I was concerned. This was all off the record, but Jorge and I sat down in his classroom at Seawell High once to talk about how the season had gone. It was the year that Seawell

had lost the state championship to Galloway, their biggest rival, in a close battle. Jorge agreed to talk about it as long as it was off the record. He told me he thought that Sweeney had been having trouble adjusting to living alone in Seawell. His father was in the Airforce, a lieutenant I believe...or maybe it was the Navy. I'm not entirely sure. In any case, he had been transferred during the summer before Sweeney's senior year. Sweeney didn't want to leave Seawell, he told Jorge he couldn't leave. He asked Jorge to help him. In turn, Coach Mroz spoke with the family and told me that he had made an arrangement to keep Sweeney in Seawell for his last year of high school. The logistics of the deal involved Coach Mroz virtually guaranteeing that he could pull some strings and get Sweeney into Pepperdine on a baseball scholarship, and that he would serve as Sweeney's guardian for that final year in Seawell.

From what I heard, the family agreed, and Sweeney stayed and even ended up going to Pepperdine for half a year or so. He dropped out after a disagreement with the coach out there. The coach wanted him to play short exclusively, as well as batting lefty exclusively. It was a strange battle of wills from what I can gather. I always thought it was a little crazy for a coach not to want to use all the tools Sweeney could bring to a team, but politics and stubbornness and other things I don't know about must have factored into it. What resulted was Sweeney quit the team and left Pepperdine almost immediately after the start of his second semester.

Jorge Mroz had kept his end of the deal as guardian during Sweeney's senior year, but I remember people were mumbling that Jorge had never reined Sweeney in that entire year. His grades dropped somewhat, his style of play changed in my opinion, and he seemed like a different kid. In fact, I heard he was living in some shack or shed on the Farannan golf course or some such thing.

So you believe that Sweeney's parents' departure was the reason for Sweeney's change as a player and person that year?
Well, I imagine that was part of it, but there was also a lot of

pressure on him to perform in order to get that scholarship. I think, sadly and unnecessarily, Coach Mroz blames himself for Sweeney's fall from baseball grace. But I think his mother and father leaving started the ball rolling, to be perfectly honest. They were no longer around, and the logistics of the situation had Sweeney playing baseball for a reason other than pure enjoyment, and the game was no longer fun for him. He was still the leader of that baseball team and all the players respected him, but he no longer played with that unadulterated joy the players and coaches and fans were accustomed to. People came to watch him play, and they were rarely disappointed. He was an exciting player, defensively and offensively.

Just how good was he? You've covered the Red Sox single-A team as well as the Red Sox major league club, could he have played professional ball?
No question. In my mind, no question. I know, barring injury, that he was a big-league caliber shortstop in the making. Red Sox and Cardinals scouts were raving about him during that final year at Seawell. However, a reliable source told me he turned down all offers by the end of that year. He didn't want to be drafted.

Really? How does a ballplayer turn down big-league offers?
I know, I know. I've often wondered the same. At first, we figured it was because Sweeney wanted to go to college, but we know now that obviously wasn't the case. And, like I said, baseball had lost its luster for the kid by the end of his senior year. Pepperdine, in my opinion, was just a gesture—he felt obligated to Coach Mroz and wouldn't go back on his word. Well, that's my theory anyway. Once he got out to Malibu, I heard he just went surfing or some such nonsense. He fulfilled his end of the deal by beginning the season with the Pepperdine team, and then took off to surf and fritter away his God-given talents.

It burns me to this day to think about it, to be honest.

In your opinion, even though you recognize Sweeney was no longer having fun while playing baseball, you believe he did wrong by leaving the game?

Listen, I was born and raised in northeastern Massachusetts just like him—just like you, right? Galloway's a blue-collar town, similar to Seawell. You know as well as I do that thousands of kids would've given their right arms to have his talent, and he goes and throws it all away over some family problems, a little pressure and surfing. For the love of God! The kid was the best ball player in New England at age 17. The best! I'll never know what the hell he was thinking.

But it sounded like you had put a lot of thought into why Sweeney stopped having fun and the game seemed to become more like a job for him? I take it you're not entirely sympathetic to his reasons for quitting?

You bet I'm not! Maybe I'm being selfish here, but that kid could play. He would've made a lot of people happy if he'd kept at it. Seawell is a hardcore sports town, and he was the best athlete to come out of here in decades. I don't know what was going on, really, but I think he blew it. He threw it all away and disappointed a lot of his friends, family, coaches and fellow players.

Did you ever follow up with his family to try and find out what had become of Sweeney at Pepperdine?

Well, I tried to interview Sweeney and he wouldn't return my calls to the Pepperdine program. I spoke with his mother and father briefly, but they refused to say anything. They were livid that he had quit and disappeared, but I don't think Sweeney had a good relationship with his parents to begin with—even while they all lived in Seawell together. The coach at Pepperdine, I forget his name, he crucified Sweeney when I talked to him—so much so, I didn't feel I could publish any of his quotes in *The Seawell Times*. He was fairly brutal about the whole thing. He called Sweeney a selfish player and other things along those lines—accused him of not being a team player. And as I've said, Sweeney epitomized the concept of team—whether he was playing happy or angry baseball—so I didn't trust the coach's assessment of Sweeney's character. And this is from the guy who wouldn't let Sweeney switch-hit, so I think he was a little batty to begin with. I kept my last report about Sweeney dropping out fairly vague and inconclusive in *The Seawell Times*, I didn't want to add to the rumblings and rumors circulating in town.

Since then, I've heard Sweeney's had his problems with his mental health and so on, and I suppose that might explain some of his actions back then, but I'll never understand what happened. I'm just hurt and disappointed that his talents went to waste, that a scholarship was wasted on him.

I wanted to follow his career through the major leagues, I wanted to root for a Seawell guy up at the plate at Fenway someday. Imagine for a second if the starting shortstop for the Sox was from Seawell! This town would've canonized Sweeney. He would've been a walking, talking legend. I would've done my part to make that happen, too. I would've done my best to bring that kid into the limelight he deserved. I never got my chance, and I think a lot of people in Seawell feel the same way.

You know, I hear what you're saying, and I've heard a few people talk about the whole Pepperdine thing, but it seems to me that Sweeney has become a legend of sorts in Seawell anyway.
Well, the whole "Fifteenth-Hole Incident," the City Tourney victory, and the rumors of his insanity and jailtime and all of that has gotten him some local notoriety, but I'm talking about national attention here. Listen to what I'm saying, this little coastal city, just north of nowhere, would've had a born-and-bred professional baseball player to prop up and adore!

Well, I see your point but it seems to me that was just what Sweeney didn't want. From what people are telling me, he often kept to himself and followed his own path so to speak…
Oh, don't give me that "and I took the road less traveled" b.s. Sweeney wrote some poems and pulled some pranks and lived in the out-of-bounds area of some golf course—I've heard all the stories. And nevermind his dominance in the 110 hurdles, his

skills on the track paled in comparison to what he could do on the baseball diamond. The diamond is where it would've paid off for that kid. *He wrote and traveled and did what he wanted*, blah, blah, blah—it doesn't matter. Maybe if he'd have listened to his coaches and family and followed through at Pepperdine he wouldn't have jumped off the Pennacook. He burned a lot of bridges by dropping that free ride, then he climbed one and threw it all away. The kid's dead and he doesn't deserve any more attention. He blew it, plain and simple, and plenty of people in this town feel the same as I do. Tough cookies.

Are we done here?

CASING MY LOT

I watch, unsteady, in the sweep and glare
of headlights as a stray unfurls itself
from folds of deep sleep
in the gutter's dust.
The only paved street in town is pale orange
under patches cast by weak streetlamps.
Four men welcome a fifth to their corner
with a proffered swig of sugarcane booze.
A few slowly fold their T-shirts and tanktops
up to their chests, rub their brown bellies,
whistle and laugh.
                    It never ceases,
this warm onshore wind never ceases
nudging the blown waves' mumblings
through the orange dark—a blurred song
that sways me in the street.
I think about another beer, but let it go
with a slow, unseen wave of my hand.
I turn toward bed,
barefooted amblings in the dust,
as the markets and bamboo shacks
fade from my sight.
                    The asphalt's grown
smoother in the gutters.
I angle there each night,
casing my chosen wilderness,
shuffling through this seaside tranquility.

Somewhere below my cinderblock bedroom
there is small chaos and laughter.
For a moment, near silence:
the blurred mumblings billow my mosquito net,
shift the latticework of light
cast by the glassless windows.
More small chaos,
and a child laughs at an escaped quarter horse
clopping toward greener vacant lots.

—Sweeney

(Postmarked in Ecuador, 1997)

Chapter 10

Victory at The Cities

The following story is pretty much a standard in the bars of Seawell. Everyone you meet has heard it. Almost everyone tells it differently—embellished, exaggerated, or just filled with flat-out lies. I went back to the source, Gerald Francis, for a firsthand account (well, Walt again did most of the talking) of what went down that day on the golf course.

Gerald, no one has ever been able to find Sweeney guilty of pulling all those pranks at the City Tournaments. Do you know Sweeney pulled these pranks for sure?
Gerald: *(Just nods.)*

I figure you and your son are two of the most reliable witnesses to what happened that day when Sweeney won the Cities. Can you guys help me out with some details?
Walt: Not a problem. We had fun talking to you last time. So I'll try and remember what me and my father saw that last day of the Cities.

My father says that Sweeney never said a word about the pranks for a couple of years, but all of us from Farannan kinda knew Sweeney pulled them. I mean, who else could've? The one from when he won the Cities, when he beat Crasspus, was even better than the "Fifteenth Hole Incident."

Wait, Sweeney won the Cities over Crasspus?
Gerald: *(Leaning in close to me whispering.)* He made Crasspus look like a fool that year. A fifteen-year-old kid was beating Crasspus by a stroke going into the fifteenth hole.
Walt: Yeah, Crasspus was pretty broken up by that point of the tournament. They were paired together as the leader group that last day. And, again, that year the last day was at Farannan. Every time Crasspus birdied a hole, Sweeney would birdie the next— like spring following winter, it was guaranteed. The gallery was huge that year. None of that fifty-guys-hoping-Crasspus-lost stuff from a couple years before. There were at least five hundred people following those two from hole to hole. It was the best Cities of all time. Everyone was drinking and it was a beautiful day in

June. Dad, what was that old song that everyone was singing after Crasspus and Sweeney would hit their shots from the tee?
Gerald: *(Squints in an effort to recall, then smiles and whispers)* "Molly Malone." It was "Molly Malone."
Walt: Oh yeah, that's the title. I never remember the title, I can always only remember the "cockles and mussels, alive, alive-ohh" chorus. Yeah, so, everyone would launch into that song right after those two guys would hit their drives. We'd all sing it as loud as we could right up until one of them got ready to hit their second shot. It was such a great day, I'll never forget it. Dad and Ma and Jaime and Jason and me were all there. It's the only time we all went to watch the Cities after Dad stopped playing.

Remember, Dad? Ma even turned a blind eye to all of the Miller Lites I drank that day. Unbelievable, huh Dad?
Gerald: *(Smiles and whispers in my direction.)* If you knew my Kathy you'd be amazed at that tidbit right there.
Walt: Yeah, Ma gives me a look even now when I have more than one beer when I visit.

So what happened that day, how did Sweeney beat Crasspus?
Walt: Oh yeah, sorry. Back to the golf. Well, Sweeney was just a kid with shaggy black hair and, oh I almost forgot to tell you this, the kid wasn't wearing golf shoes. It was driving Crasspus crazy, he wasn't wearing shoes at all. Completely bare foot, wearing a pair of grey surf trunks and a blue and white Hawaiian shirt. Zephyr and Mount Pheasant had made Sweeney wear spikes for the two rounds on their courses, but Farannan was his home course so they let him play how he wanted. Everyone knew it would drive Crasspus crazy, too. By the tenth hole, after those two had traded off birdie after birdie, I heard Crasspus muttering to himself. I couldn't make out what he was saying, but it didn't sound friendly. Finally, after Crasspus made a nice up-and-down from the bunker to the left of twelve's green, and we had started singing again, he yelled, "Oh, shut up! Just shut up! None of you even know what a damn 'cockle' is anyway!" That actually did quiet us down for a minute, until my brother Jason yelled, "You're the effing cock-le, Crasspus!" It was a classic moment.

Gerald: *(Lauging and muttering to himself)* Hmmpf, cock-le, Crasspus was the biggest cock-le I've ever known.

So what happened, when did the other prank happen exactly?
Walt: *(Still laughing)* Sorry, I don't want to lose it on you like last time we talked. Umm, well, I guess it started at the tee on number fourteen and it continued all the way up to the tee on the seventeenth. See, Farannan is kind of shaped like a, whaddyacallit? A parallelogram...no, wait, I mean a trapezoid. Yeah, a trapezoid. I'm breakin' out high school geometry for you, so you know you're getting a good story! Right, Dad?
Anyway, the clubhouse is at the base, at the wider end of the course, between the beach and harbor. The right, left and top sides of the trapezoid are the woods—mostly sweetrey oak and stag pine trees—that surround the course. Sweeney supposedly lived back in those woods somewhere when he was older, but as a kid he had run around and played in them until he must've known them like the back of his hand. And the fourteenth tee makes up the top right corner, at what would be the smaller end of the trapezoid.

So, at this point, as Crasspus and Sweeney came to the tee on the fourteenth, they had the woods on their right and behind the tee. It's shaded and usually damp down in that corner, kind of a weird spot on the course. Anyway, Crasspus had birdied the thirteenth hole so he was up first on the fourteenth tee. All of us in the gallery were along the back of the tee and gathered along the edge of the trees. We were quiet as Crasspus teed up and then he began a casual practice swing. When his club reached the peak of his backswing, above his head, there was this bloodcurdling scream from somewhere in the trees behind us. Crasspus nearly jumped out of his spikes, and the whole gallery was frozen with fear. I heard about a dozen people say, "What the hell was that?" Like three or four little kids started bawling. I instantly got chills from the sound of that scream.

Crasspus was freaked out, but he figured it was some drunk guy or girl or someone in the gallery. The officials came up on the tee and asked everyone to please be quiet while the golfers were on the tee or they'd stop serving beer on the course or some crap like that. Everyone was looking at each other in the gallery.

A minute or so passed, and Crasspus stood behind his ball and looked up toward the green. I think he had a seven iron or something like that in his hand. It was one of the two par threes on the course. He seemed annoyed but not too flustered, and so he lined up his club behind the ball and did his stupid little butt-wiggle that he did before every swing. He started his backswing, and I swear to God there wasn't a peep coming out of that gallery. None of us even cleared our throats, or moved an inch (partly in fear of the beer being cutoff, and partly because we were scared of that damned noise). His club gets to the peak of his backswing and there was the scream again! It sounded like a demon was screaming "*Haaaay-ulllllll!*" It sounded exactly like the word "hell" had been screamed by a demon in the trees.

Everyone there, even the officials, knew it did not come from the throat of a human being. Nothing human could scream that loud with such a high, strange, bloodcurdling pitch.

What did Crasspus do?
Gerald: *(Softly)* He topped his shot. A real worm-burner!
Walt: A "worm-burner" is when someone just hits the top of their ball and it flies low and skips along the ground before rolling to a stop. Crasspus had hit it about seventy-five yards along the ground.

Again, he was nearly pulling his repaired hair plugs out of his head with how mad he was. It was strange. No one in the gallery was even laughing, because we were all kind of disturbed by the sound of that scream.

The officials stopped play for a short time while they searched the woods, but they didn't find any sort of stereo speakers or any person or demon hiding out there. We all knew it was no one in the gallery because the noise was so loud that we would have run away from whoever was making it if they had been in the crowd. But it was definitely coming from the woods.

The officials came back, and Sweeney was instructed to

tee up. Crasspus moaned and complained, but Sweeney just went up there and asked him to step aside. He teed up his ball, and everything went silent. I'll never forget it, we were all standing there around the tee, lining the trees—five or six hundred of us not even sipping at our beers. If you can picture the crowd around Sweeney in the shape of a giant V, I was standing at the top right of the V looking toward the bottom center where Sweeney stood behind his ball. He had a six iron, I think. He addressed the ball and was going to swing away without a practice swing. He starts his backswing, and I noticed a bunch of people with their hands over their ears, wincing. Sweeney gets to the top of his swing and, "Haaaay-ulllllllll!" It was clear, violent, and timed perfectly with the peak of his backswing.

The crowd kind of groaned, but Sweeney somehow came through and struck his ball just fine. He hit it to the front of the green, about twenty feet from the pin. He left himself a tough putt, but at least he had hit the damn thing despite the grotesque scream.

And Crasspus's standing there, his face has gone white, his mouth hanging wide open under that silly "Magnum-P.I." moustache he had.

There was a delayed, half-hearted cheer from the crowd. Nobody knew what the hell was going on.

Gerald: *(Laughing and waving Walt on.)*

Walt: *(Laughing, but with a serious look in his eye.)* It was the strangest feeling, knowing that noise was coming and not being able to stop it. No one knew what was screaming like that. The officials ordered Crasspus and Sweeney to keep playing. They finished the hole without another sound from the woods. Both of them made par on that hole, I think. Yeah, they tied, because I remember that Crasspus kept honors on the next tee.

Crasspus teed up his ball. And the tee on the fifteenth is right back next to the woods again—he looked a little hesitant as he started a casual practice swing. He brought the club back only halfway, and then through—nothing, no sound. He brought the club up around three-quarters and then through—nothing, no noise at all. It was funny as hell, because the whole crowd was quiet, just watching Crasspus test the waters. We were all kind of relieved at the second practice swing, because no one wanted to hear that scream again.

I guess Crasspus felt confident that whatever had made the noise behind the fourteenth tee had not followed us to the fifteenth. I thought we were clear of it too, to be honest. He addressed his ball, and we were all perfectly quiet staring up at him on the elevated tee. He started his backswing. My mother grabbed my arm and buried her head in my chest. I was this close (shows me the length of an inch between his thumb and index finger) to doing the same to my father who was standing next to me. And at the apex of his damn backswing, "Haaaay-ulllllll!" It was uncanny. I got the chills again, and some people started to laugh quietly as Crasspus's Titleist Four hooked deep into the woods—we all heard it drill a tree trunk with a loud knock! Crasspus just stood there, petrified with rage, then he slammed his club into the ground.

Sweeney teed up. He didn't take any practice swings, he had his three wood out and he was going for the green. Remember, this is the infamous fifteenth hole of the infamous "Fifteenth-Hole Incident" two years before. And the gallery was silent. My mother was past the point of watching, she had turned her back and covered her ears at this point—like a bunch of other people in the crowd. Pretty funny sight, actually. Little kids were crying, teenagers sipped nervously at their beers trying to look like they weren't scared, my Dad looked like he was sweating bullets—just chewing away at his fingernails.

Gerald: *(Looking at me earnestly and whispering)* That bird made a dreadful sound, you would have sweat bullets too, Owen...

Wait, it was a bird that was screaming? How do you know that?
Walt: *(In mock anger)* Jeez, Dad, I try to tell the story how you told me to and you go and mess it up. What the heck? C'mon now, that's not right.
Gerald: *(Whispering)* I'm sorry, I'm sorry. You're right, you're doing a good job. I broke my own cardinal rule, I'm sorry. Go on, tell it.

Go on Walt, you were saying Sweeney was about to hit his ball off the tee.
Walt: OK, I'll try *(Shoots a dirty look at his father, then shakes his head and smiles)*. So Sweeney starts his backswing, my mother's not looking and my father's losing weight next to me. He has this slow, controlled, graceful backswing and it reaches its peak and a spine-tingling "Haaaay-ulllllll!" comes out of the trees beyond Sweeney. Right after the "Haaaay-ulllllll!" we all hear the thwack of the club on the ball, and then the whole gallery is silent until the ball lands on the front of the green, two-hundred-and-twenty-odd yards away—and it's pin-high, five feet to the right of the hole! Somebody, I wish I knew who, launched the whole crowd right into the loudest "Molly Malone" of the day just a moment after Harold Crasspus began complaining. We were singing "Molly Malone" that year, for some reason or other. I've already said that, haven't I?

Yeah, well anyway, Crasspus' whinings were drowned out, and the spell of the "Haaaay-ulllllll!" had been lifted by Sweeney's pin-high shot. Kids were laughing, jumping and tackling each other in the rough, teenagers were shot-gunning their beers and paying up on bets, adults were singing at the top of their lungs. It was crazy, I mean, most of those people have never even golfed in their life. They just wanted to see Sweeney beat Crasspus. The whole crowd of us marched down the left side of the fairway, singing and cheering Sweeney on.

And then we all stopped in dead silence about halfway to the green, because this little bluish bird with a long neck came fluttering out of the woods. It came down from one of the low branches in one of the stag pines. It opened up a gigantic, shiny, green tail with the blue, iridescent eyes at the end of every feather, and gave one more "Haaaay-ulllllll!" for good measure. It was a freakin' peacock!

Everyone, except Sweeney, had stopped singing and stood still. It was near perfect silence. I remember my sister said, "Must've escaped from Benson's Animal Farm, huh?" Benson's was an old zoo that was shut down by then, so it didn't make sense but not much did at that point.

Sweeney was up ahead and he simply kept strolling toward the green with his putter in his hand, singing "Alive, alive oh-oh, alive, alive oh-oh...." quietly to himself, "crying cockles and mussels, alive, alive-oh-oh."

All six hundred of us were staring at the bird, stock still, and then it closed its tail and strutted off into the underbrush. I kept looking at the bird and then up at Sweeney walking toward the green, and then back at the bird. I glanced at my father and he was just starting to laugh. And as he started losing it, everyone else was quiet, and Crasspus looked like he was going to keel over and pass out.

We all heard a soft commotion of feathers, and then nothing. Not another sound was heard from the woods.

That is, until Sweeney reached the top of his backswing on the sixteenth tee along the eastern edge of the course. Again, there was a "Haaaay-ullllllll!" and, again, Sweeney hit it straight down the fairway.

Gerald: *(Smiling and shaking his head and whispering)* I don't know how the kid hit it straight with that damn bird screamin' away up in the trees.

And that was it? The bird was gone?

Walt: Well, that's the thing. After the sixteenth, the last two holes aren't bordered by the woods, so the bird was pretty far away. Every so often the bird screamed "Haaaay-ullllllll!" off in the distance but it only caused laughter by that point. I remember some high school kids had already started pounding a beer every time they heard the bird's cry—you know how Seawell kids will make a drinking game out of just about anything.

Anyway, the officials were somehow inclined to believe that Sweeney had something to do with the bird—that he had somehow trained a peacock to follow the golfers from the woods along the fourteenth, fifteenth and sixteenth holes. But, I mean, how could someone train a peacock to scream at a specific point in a golfer's backswing? It's seems impossible to me. And Crasspus was past the point of coherent speech on the subject. He was fuming and gargling like he was having a seizure or something. No one ever even pinned the 200-golf-balls-on-the-green trick, that "Fifteenth-Hole Incident" thing, on Sweeney from a couple years before, so I don't see how they could pin the peacock thing on him like that.

Gerald: *(Pulling me close and whispering in my ear)* I'm not gonna tell you how he did it, but Sweeney explained it all to me, but made me swear not to tell anyone. I had to pester him to tell me every time I saw him for a few months, but he finally explained it all. That kid could do anything he set his mind to, and that's the god-honest truth. You can put that in your book *(with a wink)*.

Walt and Gerald went on to tell me that even though the officials of the 45th Annual Seawell City Golf Tournament felt Sweeney was responsible for the peacock, they were unable to prove it. According to Gerald, when asked about the bird and the "Fifteenth-Hole Incident" of a few years previous, Sweeney only smiled beatifically and twice repeated, "I will neither confirm nor deny the allegations at hand."

At the awards banquet that evening, a fifteen-year-old, smirking, barefoot Yardbird Sweeney politely refused the winner's trophy—further embarrassing Harold Crasspus, who snatched the trophy and stormed off the deck above the ninth green as the crowd again began singing and laughing through one final chorus of "Molly Malone."

OUTSIDE THE GREEN CITY

In low shadows above the leaf-thronged floor
the ghostly, domed mushrooms hold quiet court.
A warbling copse of emerald ferns leans and bends
beneath currents and floods of summer light.
Uphill, under an eleven-o'clock sky,
green depths of forest are flayed-through and mottled
with sharp, gold sunlight. I'm watching your dark
eyes shine through the shade of trees drenched with moss.
Softly, in morning light, spiderwebs billow
as copper dragonflies flit, dart and spark.
They shine—struck flints amid the silken luff.

And the soft peak of my upper lip is adrift
on the cooled edge of the petal of your ear.
Your dark irises are bluegreen coronas:
lidded and lashed reflections of the forest's
late-August, sun-ignited canopy.

—Sweeney

A SOFT DAY

I am of smoke
this paleskinned morning—
the tinge of it
lifts from my mist-damp clothes.
We warm one another with a drawn-
out embrace, good-byes
through the soft lull
of your syllables.
And the waves insist.
The waves insist,
as they did at midnight
beneath a veil of blown mist
held back by our driftwood fire.

You are of mist
this paleskinned morning—
the tinge of it
lifts the last flecks
of firelight from your green eyes,
sets the smell of smoke
in your nightdark hair.
A drawn-out embrace;
the soft lull
of your lips on my lips.
And the waves insist.
The waves insist
we were torsos of smoke,
entangled limbs of mist.

—Sweeney

(This poem and "Outside the Green City," arrived typed on separate
sheets of onionskin paper, mailed in the same envelope from Venezuela in
1996.)

CHAPTER 11
SEQUEL TO "THE STING"

My father, Patrick Kivlin, and Sweeney were childhood friends, and Sweeney trusted my father with stories he wouldn't share with anyone else. My father is six feet tall, with a sandy tangle of hair. He always looks as if he's just gotten out of the ocean and towel-dried his head.

He was forty-four years old, ten years older than Sweeney, at the time of the writing of this letter—still in good surfing shape and proud of that fact. He was born and raised in Seawell, just as his mother and father were. As I've mentioned before, he grew up surfing and fishing, playing any and all sports, and generally spending as much time as possible outdoors by the ocean or on a playing field with Yardbird Sweeney.

Owen,

I've decided it would be best if I wrote this story out for you. It's really many stories lumped together, because Sweeney told me this whole thing in bits and pieces over the span of about six or seven years. I found I had to write it out by hand. My thoughts and memories seem to be explained best through the pace of writing in longhand.

I've included some of the details that Goatboy Obregon and Jay Scanlann passed on to me about the ice cream truck hijacking. But I know the story well enough to tell it to you, so I'm just gonna let it fly.

Sweeney had been very careful to cover his tracks and to make sure that no one suspected him of even a modicum of sanity before he started explaining any of this to me. That being said, I suppose the statute of limitations is up on any and all of the frauds and crimes I'm about to detail—so I don't feel too badly in finally telling this story.

Now, I should say that Sweeney always began the installments of this long story the same way. He'd look me in the eye, usually over a couple bottles of Harp and say something along the lines of: "Remember, Paddy, I don't recommend getting arrested and making an effort to be diagnosed insane as a valid career path for everyone. Who knows," he'd say, "someday, maybe it'll be the right one for you? I mean, I'll tell you how I pulled all this off because it's good to have options, right?"

Basically, Sweeney had spent sixteen months or so stuck in the Merritt House of Corrections writing, reading and doing push-ups. He told me he sat in his cell for most of that time and memorized the necessary symptoms he would need to practice in order to be diagnosed with Schizoaffective Disorder, Bipolar Type. I remember this is what he was aiming for because I eventually went down to the Wallace Library [Seawell's Public Library] and read up on it myself. I read up on all the disorders in the *DSM-IV*, it's sort of a cookbook filled with recipes for insanity. I also studied the *DSM-IV Casebook*. I found that Sweeney had done his homework, and that he seems to have imitated insanity with aplomb.

Sweeney didn't go to college, but he'd taken some classes here and there and done a ton of reading and writing on his own. Sweeney always called his jail time, "my study-abroad semester at Merritt." I think his jail time actually did help him figure out what he wanted to do with himself when he got out. He found out that being crazy, legally, doesn't necessarily mean that you are a danger to society. I think he told me that around three percent of *sane* people in the U.S. react violently to situations involving stress. He got the whole idea to become legally insane because he read that that number, that percentage, is exactly the same for the population of *insane* people in the U.S. He realized that being an insane person didn't mean you were violent. "This might have its benefits," he always told me. He realized that the supposed scientists in charge of dishing out those benefits were a predictable bunch, as well. In a stroke of luck, it hadn't hurt that the prison psychiatrist was a childhood friend of ours.

These facts encouraged Sweeney, as well as his rationalization that working in some damn cubicle for forty of the approximately eighty-four hours of daylight per week was the equivalent of a prison sentence. He didn't want to work a single day of his life in that environment. He always said, "Fuck that, Paddy. I'm never doing that shit and you and me both know that most of the hamsters stuck in their cubicles would get out for good if they could just figure out how to do it, right?" I had to kind of agree with him. He said that sort of thing to me all the time, as if he wasn't quite sure if he could justify what he'd done in his own conscience.

But Sweeney knew he didn't want to return to Merritt in the future either, so he devised a crime that would most likely lead a judge or any competent psychiatrist to believe he was legally insane, but harmless to society. He was hoping to receive a monthly stipend from the government while doing some kind of non-stressful volunteer work and then sneaking off for a surf trip a few times a year.

Sweeney told me he realized his scheme would take a very long time to put into place. He said he started showing signs of his symptoms in the last two months of his time in Merritt, and then he waited about two years to commit the crime that would eventually get him a stipend from the government so he could travel and write.

O., you were just a little kid when Sweeney served his time, probably five or six years old. Sweeney had really done a number on that Mormon kid's jaw. I knew that, and he knew that, and he was sorry for it. He felt he deserved his time in Merritt, and he told me his brawling days were over—that he would never fight anyone again. And he was telling me the truth, because I never heard about him getting in any fights after he got out of Merritt. He grew up quick during his short stay in prison.

But Sweeney was a shrewd study and he decided to use that remorse, as genuine as it was, to his advantage. He told me that when the day came where it was exactly two months until his release from Merritt he made an appointment to see the prison psychiatrist, Dr. Karen Bent. Sweeney and I had gone to kindergarten with her at the Oakland. She moved to Duxbury or somewhere after that, around first or second grade, but we'd all been friends as little kids. Dr. Bent is a good doctor and a good person. Sweeney went in to see her that day and he told her in graphic detail what he'd done to the Mormon kid and how awful he felt. She asked him what prompted his confession and remorse and he said a little voice told him to talk to her that day.

He started in on the bid to become legally insane right away. He told her he'd just heard that little voice for the first time in his life that morning, while eating his scrambled eggs. She thought the whole thing was very interesting. Karen and I have never really talked about their meetings, due to that doctor-patient privilege thing. But Sweeney told me all about their sessions in detail.

His behavior in her office was cool, calm and collected, although he told me how he continually asked to borrow her mechanical pencil to jot down notes in a little notebook. Whenever she wrote something down, he asked to borrow the pencil and he started to write something down. "For my poems," he kept telling her. But he kept breaking the tip of the pencil and handing it back to her apologetically as if he didn't know how to work the thing. He was in the office for an hour or so, and he said he must've broken the lead on that pencil twenty-five times. Dr. Bent has a great poker face, but Sweeney could tell her interest was piqued. Four weeks later, one month before his release, he purposely caught Dr. Bent's attention again. This time he began responding to the supposed voice he heard.

He was in the cafeteria and he threw his oatmeal on the floor. He was talking to himself like he was frustrated. A guard named Leo Luque, who we went to high school with, brought him to Dr. Bent. Leo was a good guy too, funny and tough as hell when we were growing up. Sweeney described to me how gently Leo had escorted him down the hall. And then he left him with the doctor. Growing up, we'd never seen Leo be gentle, so that was sort of hard for me to picture, but Sweeney swore Leo, one of the toughest guys in Seawell, had a gentle side.

Anyway, that day, Sweeney told Dr. Bent that the voice he heard kept saying, "Check him out, he's having his oatmeal now isn't he? There it is, he'll finally have his oats." He explained to Dr. Bent, in a calm and collected manner, that he hadn't heard the voice since the last day he'd been to her office—exactly one month previous. He told her that the voice repeatedly insinuated that he was learning some sort of lesson, and that his oatmeal was his medicine. He told the good doctor that he would no longer eat oatmeal, "even if it was cinnamon raisin." He expressed his need to get out of Merritt and he told her he felt he'd been cooped up too long.

I guess Dr. Bent took some notes and seemed very interested and perplexed. Sweeney saw the doctor just once before his release four weeks later. He told her he hadn't heard the voices anymore, and that he'd eaten all his oatmeal for two weeks. She seemed happy for him, Sweeney said, and they didn't see each another for about two years.

Sweeney got out of Merritt on the day the swell from that no-name storm peaked in Seawell. Leo Luque somehow got him out a couple hours early because he knew how much Sweeney wanted to get in the water before the tide got too high. Leo was very good to him in there, and Sweeney appreciated it. First thing Sweeney did was go surfing. He told me how he'd seen Micky Obregon that morning, but he'd purposely acted a little flighty to benefit his cause. He told me how he felt bad, because it was really good to see Mick again and he wanted to thank him for sending him all those surf magazines while he was locked up. But Sweeney acted a little haunted that morning because he knew he had to stay disciplined and stick to his symptoms in order for the whole thing to eventually work.

(This portion of the letter is written in a hurried scrawl.)

Owen, hold on a minute...Sorry, I just ran down to check the waves because it sounded like the wind had died. I'll have to continue this letter later. It's head high and glassy with only Goatboy in sight. I'll go surf with him and maybe have some beers afterwards at The Wardin, if he's up for it. Talk to you in a little while, I'll be sure to grab a long right for you....Okay, I'm back. Me and Mick had a great surf at Seawell. It was mid-tide coming in and so, about a half-hour after I paddled out, the sandbar over on the south side of the Little Rocks started working. I rode my Lis fish, the one I traded for out in San Diego a few years ago. It was perfect, just enough push and hollowness to the waves. We both got some good ones and then we went to the Wardin for a few. I had four or five beers with Goatboy , K.J. and Dicky LaFerrier so it might be hard for me to get back on track.

You know what? On second thought, I'll get back to this Sweeney stuff after I sleep this buzz off. I don't want to start running my mouth through this pen too much.

Let's see, where was I? I guess it was two years from the time Sweeney got out of Merritt to the time he stole the ice cream truck. He pretty much lived out in the woods in the spring, summer and fall during those years. Those were the years when you and Sweeney used to play catch and tag and all those imaginary games you two made up together in our backyard near the golf course. The two of you were best friends for a while there. I remember watching him teach you how to climb and identify trees and you taught him how to tie his shoes, unaware that he knew how to do that already. I wonder how much of that you remember.

Sweeney mostly worked with the Goatboy during that time, doing tree work and plantings. Everyone in Seawell was beginning to wonder about him, and they thought he had already been a little wacky before he went into Merritt — so by then they figured he was beyond the point of no-return. Even I'd had my doubts about Sweeney. He had changed so much while he was away. But when I'd watch him playing with you out back, I knew he was doing fine. I told anyone who'd ask about him that he was okay, but no one really believed me. They just wanted to hear more gossip. Seawell's a good-sized city but it operates like a small-town gossip circuit most of the time.

I didn't know it at the time, but Sweeney knew he still had to solidify the idea of being loony in the minds of a lot of people in order to eventually get those checks from the government. His hair had grown long and he had a huge, nappy beard going. I thought it was all par for the course, really — but that's coming from a close friend of his. A lot of the conservative sorts in Seawell, the same people who were still angry with Sweeney for supposedly wasting his scholarship to Pepperdine, thought his hair and beard and overall ragged appearance was a sign that he had gone crazy while he was locked up. Goatboy didn't care about Sweeney's appearance because he was his best tree guy and he was reliable — unlike most of the crackheads that worked for him.

There they were, all of Goatboy's crackhead laborers, trying so hard to be sane — just trying to get by. They were failing painfully — poor guys — while Sweeney was trying to be more and more crazy as the days went by, knowing he would be rewarded for it. It was a strange situation to witness, especially since none of us really knew the reality of what was going down at the time.

Goatboy told me how most of the crackheads never made it to work and were basically spaceshots when they did show up. Sweeney didn't drink or go to the bars much during that time — I suppose he was saving money to travel. He just wrote, surfed, hid in the woods, played some barefoot golf in the evenings by himself, worked for Goatboy and grew a lot of hair. Once in a while, I'd hear of a mild fit he'd throw while at work and Goatboy would get worried and take him back to the Kemp Aaberg to "chill out for a couple days." Not a bad life. If it weren't for Seawell's long, cold winters Sweeney would've probably kept on doing what he was doing, too. But he needed money to travel and surf in the winter and the Schizoaffective thing seemed like the best way to do it.

After letting his appearance slip a little, Sweeney started messing around with the crackheads' minds whenever Goatboy wasn't around. He insisted that they called him "King Sweeney" and Goatboy told me he once heard Sweeney tell the crackheads, "Hell, I have hollow bones, fellas. I could fly around and do all this tree work, but then none of us would get any overtime would we?" None of the crackheads wanted to do any of the sketchy tree work, so Sweeney would do it while telling them not to worry because he could always fly away if he started to fall. After a while, he was pretty much the reason most of those guys quit working for Goatboy. Sweeney freaked them out, but don't tell Goatboy because he'd lose it if he heard that.

Eventually, Mick started hearing about Sweeney wanting to be called "King" and stuff and he got a little worried. I remember Goatboy coming over and telling me how Sweeney talked about the voices he was hearing in his head. He'd told Goatboy he'd heard them since the last few days of his stay in Merritt. Sweeney was lying to Goatboy, and felt bad about it, but he had to keep up the appearances to make it all work. Besides, Goatboy has a big mouth to be honest—and sanity was not really a factor in their friendship, anyways. They surfed and drank together, and Sweeney showed up for work regularly. That was good enough for both of them back then.

During the winters of those couple of years Sweeney would take off for Ecuador and other South American surf spots. He always said he nearly froze his stones off that one winter when he lived in his boat out in the woods. He swore he wouldn't do it again. He'd come back later and later in the spring each year. There was one year where he didn't come back until late August, and he was raving about a little spot down by the Guatemalan border—a righthand pointbreak with a sand bottom. He just raved about it, and said the summer south swells hit it just right for weeks on end. I was a little jealous of all the surf he was getting back then, but I had a family to raise so I sort of lived vicariously through him, I suppose.

I was starting to get worried that Sweeney wasn't going to come back, and he seemed to be acting more strangely each time I would see him. The only sign of his sanity was his friendship with you, Owen. You took him for what he was, and the two of you were like best friends back then. I noticed how fewer and fewer adults took the time to hang out with Sweeney in those years, and how he spent more and more time with you in our backyard and out on the course in the summer evenings.

I remember getting a little upset, myself, at how Sweeney was sort of pulling away from all of us. But he'd always take the time to tell me about where he'd traveled and what waves he'd surfed and how his writing and Spanish were coming along. I didn't want to pressure the guy toward any sort of normal life because I could see that he was happy. He seemed to be pulling away from supposed "adult society" but he seemed almost content—strange and lonesome, but content. Does that make any sense?

I figured that there weren't many people in his life in the

first place, especially after all that stuff he went through after leaving Pepperdine. He'd lost his girlfriend and cousin Tommy who was one of his oldest friends, and his parents were definitely out of the picture at that point. And on top of all that, he goes away for a while to Merritt then comes out and seems happy— crazy, but happy.

It's a weird thing to see someone who is genuinely happy, you know? I don't think most people in Seawell know how to deal with someone who figures out a way to do whatever he or she wants to do. I just wanted to keep Sweeney writing and traveling back then, it seemed it was what he needed to do. I tried to ignore the protective instincts I had for him as an old friend. It was hard for me sometimes, but I think Sweeney appreciated it.

I know for sure, in the long run, he still looked at me as one of his best friends. The day he started telling me about the ice cream truck hijacking was the day I knew that he trusted me like a brother. I mean, if anyone had found out about any of this he would've been back at Merritt in a heartbeat—for a much longer stay, too. It was hard for Sweeney to trust anyone after what his parents did to him. I think you already talked to Sweeney's cousin Tommy about that situation. That's why I say it took a long time for Sweeney to trust me entirely.

So, eventually, this is what he told me he did to sort of seal the deal with the diagnosis of Schizoaffective, Bipolar. I'll try to be as detailed as I can. It shouldn't be too hard for me, because this is absolutely my favorite Sweeney story—and that guy told me a lot of damn stories.

In any case, it was late August and Sweeney knew that this big festival was happening during Labor Day up in northern Vermont. It was in this remote mountain pasture somewhere. It was an underground sort of thing back then—something to do with sculpture, music, art and most likely drugs. It was called The Vapid Tortuga Festival, and it was different in that nobody sold anything like T-shirts or food at the festival. You just showed up, bought a ticket and supplied all your own water and food and you could barter for drugs and booze. It all lasted ten days or so, and it switched locations every year throughout the northern

Appalachian Mountains. There were all these sculptures and art-work and music featured each night on different stages and in different parts of the woods and meadows. It was a very cool setup, from how Sweeney described it. Sweeney had memorized the directions to the festival earlier that summer so he could take off for it when he got his chance. "If you're trying to look insane," he'd say, "you can't have sense enough to buy a map at a gas station—you know what I mean?" It was the little things that made his plan a success, and Sweeney had a talent for the little things in everything he did.

It was a Monday, hot as hell, and Sweeney and Goatboy were doing tree work out on Parkview Ave., near the old Capanetti house. He was sick of working and sweating and miss-ing out on the surf in Mexico, so he decided that it had been long enough. He needed to commit the crime that week in order to make it up to the festival in time. He needed to start the process of committing a crime, getting caught, going to trial, getting a diagnosis and collecting some money from the government.

And Jay Scanlann, a Seawell guy few years younger than us, was driving an ice cream truck that summer. He had permits for Seawell's beaches, and he'd made a killing with all the nice weather that July and August. Sweeney knew he'd made more than enough to go back to school, so he didn't feel too bad about stealing his truck at that time of the summer. Scanlann's parents had money anyway. Sweeney didn't know how he was going to actually steal the thing, but he was ready. So that Monday he's up in that huge seaside blackthorn on Parkview, working near the top. He sees these little kids, the Swenson and Capanetti kids I think, quietly tying cans to the ends of a long piece of fishing line. When they heard the music from the ice cream truck coming around the corner they set up the line at around car-bumper height across Parkview Ave., right before it crosses Hollyrood St.

Sweeney climbed down from the tree when he saw Scanlann driving down the street. James and Pauly Capanetti and Dave and Janet Swenson were the only little kids I ever knew who didn't like the ice cream man. Sweeney said he thought it was because they didn't have much money, and they were bored.

Irregardless, they had been screwing around with Scanlann all summer long whenever he drove through the Oaklands section of town. They attacked the poor guy with squirt-gun ambushes, snowballs saved from February, they fired bottle rockets out of whiffle ball bats at his truck—they pulled out all the pranks they could think of on Scanlann.

Scanlann told me all about the kids, and Sweeney stealing the truck, later that fall after he dropped out of the University of Chicago and came back to Seawell. Scanlann was a good guy. I used to see him down at the Wardin every so often back then. And Goatboy has told me his version of this story several times down at The Wardin as well. Everyone involved in this whole fiasco acted all pissed off back then, but I think they were all having fun chasing each other around and battling.

So, in any case, Scanlann is coming down the street in his truck, ringing his bell and making his way toward Sweeney, Goatboy and the can-trick trap. Sweeney put down all his tools in the grass and told Goatboy that Slim had commanded him to get a Snow Cone and a Fanta from the truck. "Slim" was the name he'd given to one of his hallucinations—one of the floating heads who were responsible for the voices he'd heard every day of that summer. Mick knew all about Slim.

This is how Goatboy tells me this part of the story, he seems to like the part where Sweeney and the kids were all about to wreak havoc on the truck. And Goatboy tells me this part of the story every other time I see him these days—if he has a few beers in him, which is most of the time. He's always like:

"Paddy, I'm tellin' ya, I think Sweeney knew what he was doin', he set us all up, I'm tellin' ya.

"'Cause that day I says to Sweeney, 'You hate Snow Cones. What the fuck are you talking about?'

"And Sweeney puts down his tools in the grass and he says to me, with that weird fuckin' look in his eyes, 'You just can't argue with Slim, Goatboy. Out of the five heads, he's the meanest.'

"So I says, 'Oh, Jesus Christ, you are completely fucked! Go get your damn ice cream, and then finish this beech tree.' I remem-

ber we still hadta plant that spruce out in Amesbury later that day. I wanted to get that job done, and here he is tellin' me: 'The heads said this, and Slim said that, blah, blah, blah....' And I'd been on the ground completely baked all morning, so I never saw the Capanetti and Swenson kids setting up the can trick—the little bastards."

Usually, I manage to get away from Goatboy before he continues the story, because we've all heard it from him a million times. And later, after I learned that Sweeney had all this planned out, I knew there was a whole lot more to it than Goatboy knew. Sometimes it was hard not to let Goatboy in on the whole thing, once I'd been told. He'd been friends with me and Sweeney for a long time but sometimes he runs his mouth like a teenager after a school dance, so I had to resist filling him in on the truth back then.

See, Sweeney told me he had two dollars and some change, all of it in dimes, nickels and pennies—Sweeney knew the exact amount, let's say it was $2.73—in Goatboy's dump truck. So he grabbed the $2.73 and waited a little ways past the spot where those little kids had set up the fishing line. For whatever reason, the can trick never got old to those little kids, god bless 'em. Scanlann was driving down Parkview and he's got the ice-cream-truck version of the theme song from that Paul Newman movie "The Sting" playing loud and clear. He stops ringing his bell when he sees Sweeney and he waves. Sweeney said he just stood there as if he was having a conversation with one of his talking-head hallucination friends.

Goatboy was sitting in the shade drinking some water and smoking a joint. Sweeney just kept talking and gesticulating until Scanlann drove his bumper right into the fishing line and the cans started clanking away at the sides of the truck. It was funny as hell, but Sweeney couldn't laugh—because that would show that he knew what was going on—so he just kept talking to "Slim" and the other heads while Goatboy coughed up half his water with that nasally laugh of his.

Scanlann stopped in the middle of Parkview, threw the

truck into park and jumped out. The Swensons and Capanettis popped out from behind the coldwater-ivy hedge up on the hill in the Barrett's yard. They started calling Scanlann names and laughing: "Ahh, ha, ha, ha! You suck! Get a real job, shithead!" Sweeney and Goatboy both told me that the kids were laughing hard and then they'd run twenty yards or so up toward Hollyrood Ave. and they'd stop and call Scanlann some more names. Scanlann was trying to pull the cans out of his bumper and the fishing line was all tangled in the axle and he was swearing and getting all pissed off. "The Sting" was still blaring out of the megaphone speaker on top of the truck.

Goatboy got up and starts yelling at the kids, he hates kids, and then him and Scanlann started running after them. Goatboy yelled for Sweeney to follow but Sweeney just pretended to be violently arguing with the heads about the superiority of Chipwiches over Snow Cones or something like that. Goatboy remembers that Sweeney's gestures indicated that Slim was not happy with him at that point in time.

Sweeney heard Goatboy tell Scanlann, "Forget about that crazy fuck, let's get those little bastards!" Then the chase was on. Scanlann stopped for a second at the top of the Barrett's yard and yelled down, "Sweeney, just leave the money on the dash and take whatever you want!"

That, Sweeney told me, was a better cue than he could have possibly hoped for. He got in the truck, turned up "The Sting" a little bit and drove down Parkview, onto Rogers, onto 495, toward 93 and all points North. He said he let "The Sting" play all the way out of Seawell. The fishing line snapped when he took the left onto Rogers in front of Dunkin' Donuts, and the cans fell off the truck. Sweeney put his $2.73 in a cup on the dash and kept it there for the whole trip. In fact, when he came back, the police found the cash box untouched, the ice cream all melted and rancid in the coolers of the ice cream truck. Sweeney'd left everything precisely the way he found it when he stole it.

Sweeney stayed up at the festival for about three days. When he got back he just went about his business like nothing had happened. Scanlann had called the police a day or two after

Sweeney had taken off. He'd waited for Sweeney to show up with the truck, but then the guys who he leased the truck from started breathing down his neck so he was forced to call the cops. Sweeney showed up for work on the next Tuesday, after the long weekend. Goatboy always describes him that specific morning as, "all banged up and rough around the edges. Basically, he was fucked." The cops were waiting for him to come to work and they took him away. He was back in Merritt until his trial, but they treated him with kid gloves out there—Leo Luque told me he made sure of that much.

The trial came up and the judge granted the Public Defender's request for psychological tests on Sweeney. Scanlann and Goatboy had informed the cops, when the truck was stolen, about Sweeney's odd behaviors—at that point, everyone in Seawell was worried about the guy.

So, it was back to Dr. Karen Bent for a round of interviews and tests and analysis. Sweeney told me that he made sure he had the symptoms and habits of a Schizoaffective patient down pat by then. He'd been careful of exactly how and when he'd stolen the truck. He showed no guilt about stealing the truck, he expressed that he'd been told by Scanlann that he could "take whatever he wanted." He also left that cup full of change on the dashboard and told Dr. Bent he'd paid for the use of the truck with the $2.73 in change.

Growing up, Sweeney was the craftiest, smartest person I knew. A lot of difficult things came easily to him, and so I can imagine that if he says he studied and memorized and displayed the behaviors of a person with Schizoaffective Disorder, Bipolar Type, that means he had it down to a science. Dr. Bent and the judge and everyone else in Seawell never had a chance to discover his plan if Sweeney put even a little effort into it. And, from the sound of it, he put a lot of effort into it.

Over the years, he revealed to me all the things that led Dr. Bent toward the right diagnosis: "Slim," and the hallucinated talking heads; the request to be called "King Sweeney" by the crackheads; the ongoing commentary of the voices; how the voices resurfaced on the anniversary of his release from Merritt. All these behaviors were perfectly timed and practiced parts of Manic Episodes and the other requirements for a Schizoaffective, Bipolar diagnosis.

Sweeney pulled off the perfect fraud and ended up with a few months in Darville Mental Hospital for his effort. He was released with a monthly stipend of around five or six hundred dollars. That's where Dr. Bent came through for him. She had to diagnose him as Sweeney wanted her to, he'd set her up just right, but she cut through the red tape quicker than normal for him because she'd been in Sweeney's second-grade class. I think the normal waiting period for that sort of a stipend is at least a year, maybe two. There's a lot of crap to wade through as the government drags its feet through every stage of that sort of thing. Sweeney had his money in around five or six months. So you can see, like I said, Seawell is a city that often operates like a small town—favors are plentiful if you know the right people.

After that, Sweeney lived in the out-of-bounds area of the golf course in that old trawler up on barrels, the Kemp Aaberg. He did a little volunteer work and special jobs for Goatboy—special tree work. He was instructed to avoid all stressful jobs or situations, and he was to report every six months or so to Dr. Bent for further evaluation. Sweeney told me he had trouble keeping a straight face when the doctors said, "We encourage you to avoid stressful situations and employment for several months." He said to me, " I was thinking, like, 'No fucking encouragement needed, my friends. You have my word!'"

The hard part was over for Sweeney. It had taken around three or four years from his first stint in Merritt to the time when he could take his first extended surf trip to Central America on the government's tab.

Sweeney had constructed his own reality that no one else could understand, including me. He told me he felt like a free man for the first time in his life when he was put in the mental hospital that time—ironic as that sounds.

Looking back on that, I think he meant that he was finally free to write his poems, surf the winters away in warm places and come back to Seawell during spring of each year to check in and have a few surf sessions with me and Goatboy. Sweeney had even gone far enough to have the court order me and Goatboy to be in charge of depositing his checks in his account on a monthly basis since his family wasn't around any more. And banking, apparently, was out of the question for someone in his delicate state.

We did all of this willingly because we were his oldest friends. But, as I said earlier, Sweeney seemed happy in a weird way back then—even content. And despite the label of "legally insane" he was still Sweeney, and we both were just happy he wasn't locked up in prison or an institution or working in some insurance office fifty weeks of the year. He was still Sweeney, and Sweeney was supposed to fit in our lives as a traveler and writer and surfer. We sort of needed to believe he was insane so that he could go on being the same sort of Sweeney for us.

I mean, Goatboy and I kind of lost touch with ourselves once we grew up. Maybe "lose" isn't the right way to put it. I guess I mean when you get married and have kids or own your own business you start to become someone else—a husband, a supervisor, a father—someone you haven't been before. You miss the old things a little at times. We chose our lives, and we're doing fine, but we also always liked living vicariously through Sweeney's travels.

Me and Goatboy hardly ever went on surf trips any more, we could barely get in the water around here. And while we had wives and kids we loved, we still struggled with the loss of some of the stuff that made us who we are. I'm babbling a little bit here, but I think this is why Sweeney remains a part of our lives. It's more than just fond memories of someone who's gone, some-one we haven't heard from in a long time.

It's like I've always felt that Sweeney hadn't lost any-thing as he got older. He seemed to *create* his life while my life *happened* to me and around me. There's a big difference there. Me and Goatboy always agreed that, in our opinions, the only thing Sweeney ever seemed to lose was the label of "sane." And I'm not too sure we would've ever saddled him with that label in the first place.

Looking back on all of it, knowing what I know and being the only person to really know all this stuff, I'm proud of the guy. I mean, I think he managed to find a way to get the money to do what he wanted to do. He earned his freedom.

Nobody's seen the guy in years, as far as I know, but people talk about him in the bars like he's due back any day now. Maybe it's that he's got people using their imagination as they wonder about what the hell he did with himself. I mean, he's one of us, one of the people who grew up in Seawell. He's no different, really. But, then again, he's the only one who lived in a boat out in the woods and traveled to exotic places every year and disappeared and reappeared, and maybe killed himself.

In any case, I don't think I'm supposed to understand all of it. I miss the guy and I get sad sometimes when I think about how long he's been gone, but I'm happy for him at the same time. He sort of went out on top in my mind, whether he killed himself or not. I spend a lot of time thinking about what he's done over the years, and I guess he's still around in one way or another. It still feels like he's gonna show up at the Wardin some Tuesday night. I'm pretty sure he will. My guess is that he was on his way back here one spring and then he just found a place or a person or a reason that felt like it might be a little more important to him than Seawell, his old friends and his old need to be back here.

He'll come around. He will.

CONTEMPLATING THE PENNACOOK BRIDGE

My bones grow hollow before the plunge—
as if long-lost instinct, not memory,
jogs for a stretched   instant.
It is a brief flight
upward, a soft brawl
with gravity's invisible blight.

After the crash of wind-burned flesh
on the boiling face of the currents,
innumerable bubbles rise   expire.
I was not plumed   so I plummeted.
I am not gilled   so I rise.
The twin levels of my lungs
lift me to a state of wet grace.

I am a dumb cork hefted on ebb tide.
Blackened liquid seeps from my head
above the pocked floor of the sea,
below the sieve-like expanse of night sky.

My pores are portals for the salts
and oils of my sea and my self.

—Sweeney

(Found by Miguel Obregon in the berth of the Kemp Aaberg after
Hurricane Murgill toppled the boat in 1998, just a few days after
Sweeney's bike was discovered by Seawell police under the Pennacook
Bridge. The poem was written in Sweeney's cursive in black ink on one
side of a sheet of white paper. On the other side, Micky found the final
poem in this book: "The Gealt, A Covered Bridge.")

CHAPTER 12
HURRICANE COMPANIONS

After I'd spoken to everyone and gathered all these stories together, I felt like I needed a little more closure—if that was at all possible. I decided that I would let Margaret Tierney have last word on Sweeney's whereabouts. I hoped she might be able to shed some light on the suicide-or-disappeared question. Eventually, Margaret got around to answering my original question in her roundabout, engaging way of telling a story.

The last time I saw Yardbird Sweeney was on a Saturday night in October. It was the night before Halloween, and the last belt of Indian Summer weather was moving through Massachusetts. The temperatures were up in the high sixties that weekend. The evening that I saw him was simply the most beautiful night that autumn, just wonderful weather. Farannan had closed early that year to repair the widespread damage from Hurricane Murgill in late September. Almost every hole had a tree of some kind cast across its fairway or green. The par-three number two had half of an eastern white poplar from the first fairway in its front bunker. The tree's upper branches had snapped off and sailed and tumbled nearly one hundred yards until most of them got tangled up in the sand guarding the right edge of the green. There weren't many holes that had any room to land a drive off the tee.

But I couldn't let that evening pass.

I felt winter coming on strong. Indian Summer is always too beautiful for me to ignore. I walked around the course with my clubs on my shoulder, hoping to find a few open areas to drop a few balls and hit into some of the greens—anything to help me absorb the last bit of nice weather we were going to see for a long time. I checked number three, and it was covered by the remains of Viking maples and white poplars. Five was too damp to play, it's one of the lowest points on the course so I knew it wasn't an option. Six had a huge sweetrey oak down across the middle of the fairway, but with a solid drive I felt I could clear the worst of it. I teed up and hit my shot a little low, but it made it to an open area on the fairway. This was the hole, I'm sure you've heard, from the infamous "Fifteenth-Hole Incident" with Harold

Crasspus during the Cities. It's a fun hole to play. In any case, I had about 80 or 85 yards to the pin after my first shot. Of course, I skulled a nine iron and skipped the ball over the green and down the steep, short hill into the woods behind the seventh tee. I laughed it off, dropped another ball and, of course, hit it perfectly. I still remember the shot, to this day. It landed about four feet to the right of the pin, and didn't roll more than three feet. I was ecstatic. I had a shot to remember that would tide me over through the winter months, even though it was a mulligan.

You know, just one good golf shot is all I needed to clear my head back in those days. I'd strike the ball and feel it come off the face of the iron cleanly, then the divot plops back to Earth, and I'd watch that tiny dimpled ball sail through the blue sky on the exact trajectory you hoped for headed right for that yellow flag...it's a wonderful experience, a perfect golf shot. I miss it very much, but my knees. Oh, nevermind the ramblings of a half-senile old bird like me. I'll get back to my story. I apologize.

Now, I started looking through the brush behind the green for the ball I had skulled into the woods. I wasn't looking too hard, I figured it was lost and I didn't have the luxury of Sweeney's eyes that evening. But, wouldn't you know it, I found a ball under some oak leaves. It wasn't mine, but I called it even and turned to walk back to the seventh tee to try and land a drive somewhere in the fairway that was covered by branches and leaves and looked to be pretty wet. I'd already tapped in my mulligan and fixed the divot where it had landed on the green. But as I turned to the seventh tee, all of a sudden, I saw some movement in the distance. I couldn't believe my eyes when Sweeney poked his head out from the out-of-bounds area off the right of six—the hole I had just played. He was at the base of the fallen sweetrey oak. I'd heard he was supposedly in hiding, from what I'll never know, but I ducked back down a little, behind the edge of the raised green. Sweeney looked like he was checking to see if the coast was clear, then he seemed to be studying the base of the tree where the roots were exposed from being ripped out of the ground by the wind. I still remember that he was dwarfed by the size of that tree's upended roots. He looked very small.

I had a good view of him below me, and I knew he couldn't really see me. He started walking across the fairway and then turned toward me. I ducked into the deep sandtrap that borders the back of the left side of the green and waited. After a long minute or so, Sweeney passed me, without seeing me, I'm sure of that. He then turned away from me to the northeast toward the seventh green and began walking along the edge of the woods in the rough. He walked fast, and had three old clubs leaning on his shoulder, and one ball in his left hand. He was wearing a pair of khaki shorts, a navy blue T-shirt and no shoes.

The sun had just gone down at this point, and twilight was slowly turning all the trees purple. I decided to follow him to see what he was up to. I couldn't move from the sand trap until he had walked all the way down the five-hundred-and-forty-five-yard fairway. But I saw him climb down the rocks behind the green and onto the beach. To this day I don't know why he went down to the beach, but that was my chance to get into a better hiding spot to see what he was up to.

There were small breakers crashing that night, the sound was very soothing, and a slight smell of sea spray had blown across the course. It really was a gorgeous evening, I've never forgotten it. As soon as he was out of sight, I dropped my bag of clubs and ran, as fast as an old woman in golf spikes can run, to the tunnel beneath the second tee that connects the eighth hole to the ninth tee. I guessed that Sweeney would be playing the eighth hole. It had always been his favorite on the course. It was a long par four, four hundred and sixty yards, or thereabouts, with water guarding most of the green that is tucked away to the right, as you play it, behind a hillside and some trees. It's probably the most challenging hole on the course, in my opinion. The seventh is long, and difficult too, but relatively straight without any water to worry about. The eighth is only slightly shorter with that pesky quarter-dogleg and the water that has stolen many a ball from my bag over the years. I knew Sweeney would play that hole if he was to play at all that evening.

As I covered the last several yards of my two-hundred-yard sprint (well, it would resemble more of a hurried waddling to anyone else, but to me it felt like a sprint) I made out the shape of Sweeney setting up on the eighth tee. I'd crossed the line of trees down the left side of the fairway just before he did, and I made it to my hiding spot without him seeing me. I watched him tee up the ball with an old tee he picked out of the grass. He stood directly behind it, dropped two of the clubs in his hand to the grass, addressed the ball, and hit a perfect drive without taking a single practice swing. He hit a draw, from right to left, since he's a righty. He easily cleared all the downed branches and wet leaves that cut across the fairway at about two hundred and twenty yards. His ball skipped and rolled down into the bottle-necking fairway. He hit it just far enough to get a clear shot at the green, but he had at least 180 yards left to the pin. The pin, that day, was tucked way back in the left corner of the green. The groundskeeper hadn't bothered to change the holes since the hurricane, and for some reason they hadn't pulled the flags out of the holes at that point. I suppose there was too much damage to the course itself to worry about the flagsticks. In any case, I estimate the shot Sweeney had left to be about 187 or 88 yards to the pin, and with the way that water was guarding that tiny little green behind it, I didn't think the boy had a chance.

I say "boy," but by this time Sweeney must have been at least twenty-five years old. Is that right? Twenty-five? I suppose it is, I've never really thought about it, but that seems about right. By then he'd grown out his hair and it was shaggy and long. He also wore a bushy, reddish-brown, full beard. He looked nothing like the boy I had known at fourteen. He certainly looked nothing like the eight-year-old who followed me around that course during that first summer of our friendship. As I watched the bearded Sweeney walk along the small hazels and honey ash, down the left side of the fairway it occurred to me just how much I missed the boy I knew. I was upset, more with myself, for not contacting him over the years. I wanted to walk out from behind the bluff willow I hid behind and confront the boy and see that he was okay, but I couldn't do it. I knew Sweeney had been through some difficult times after his parents moved away, after he dropped out of college that first year. I suppose I was scared that

Sweeney wouldn't talk to me, that he'd disappear into the woods if I showed myself. I'd heard he'd been to jail and to the Darville Mental Institution, I wasn't sure he would even know me any more. I would have been hurt by that, and I didn't want to be hurt.

I decided to stay put, and found myself shaking a little bit. From nervousness or my little jog to my hiding spot, I'm not sure. It was the strangest feeling. I didn't want the boy to see me and, at the same time, I couldn't take my eyes off of him.

As all this was running through my head, Sweeney approached his ball for his second shot. I was only forty or fifty yards to his right up on the hillside at this point. I had moved from the tunnel to a position behind a small bluff willow on the hill where all the kids used to sled in the wintertime. I stood stock still as Sweeney approached his ball. Through the branches, I could see that he had an old wedge, an ancient wooden driver, and a seven or eight iron in his hand. He'd left a trail of darker footprints in the tall, wet rough behind him, his pale bare feet and ankles were speckled with bits of wet grass. He dropped the wedge and the driver behind him, gripped the seven or eight iron and stared intently at the green. I doubted there was any way he could reach the green from 185 yards away. There was just a breath of wind coming off the ocean, it pushed the sea mist toward the two of us standing there in the twilight. The mist was coming in fast, and it was cooling off. There was almost a sweet sea rose smell on the air as Sweeney set up to hit his ball.

He took a moment to look back at the water, as if to gauge the breeze at his back. I saw that his green eyes were still just as clear, but now they seemed piercing rather than inquisitive. There was more of an edge to his person—a flightiness, so to speak. It was the only thing on his body that belied any sort of strain, those eyes.

As Sweeney swung his head back toward the hole, from his right shoulder toward his left, he seemed to pause as his line of sight passed the yellowed willow I was hiding behind. I hadn't moved an inch in the whole time he'd been within two hundred yards of his ball. I was so afraid that he saw me just then, in that moment, that I held my breath. I was instantly aware of the off-white stripes on my golf shirt, and the beige of my own khaki slacks. I tried to stop shaking, I had the chills for some odd reason. It was no use, I was convinced he'd seen me. I was just about to move from behind the tree, say hello and give myself up when he angled his head at the ball in front of him.

Before I could move, he was in the middle of his back-swing. He came through, slowly and rhythmically, shifting his weight firmly and with control. Even though he was on bare feet, it was as if he had golf spikes on. Everything moved with an ease and flow. His golf swing was the picture of relaxation and smoothness. Nothing was out of place. He struck the ball and turf and followed through, I let myself exhale, his divot landed on the fairway with a soft thud. He'd struck it high, and again with a slight draw from right to left.

I wasn't sure the ball would clear the large stone wall that climbed out of the far side of the pond and marked the edge of the front fringe of the green. I only moved my eyes to watch that ball, and when I glanced back at Sweeney he had already picked up his two clubs from the rough and was walking toward the hole. He wasn't even watching his shot. The ball came down pin-high, four or five feet to the right. It had enough backspin on it to roll back away from the pin about eight feet. It looked to me like the ball was just touching the edge of the fringe on the green, just above the water. He had an eight or ten-foot putt that was a little bit downhill with a slight bend to the left.

Sweeney climbed up the rise to the fringe of the green on the right side of the pond, he turned toward his ball and walked back to it. And wouldn't you know? I saw he had a pair of flip-flops sticking out of his back pocket, just like old times. I was smiling to myself, as he walked to the other side of the hole, leaving a handful of footprints on the grain of the green. He crouched and lined up the putt. He walked back across the green, removed the pin, rested it lightly on the fringe. I realized right then that Sweeney didn't have a putter with him. I wondered why, but then saw him choke down on the shaft of a club and he putted the ball with the flat face of his old, wooden driver.

It was the perfect speed, and he played the right to left break nicely. I was thrilled by what I had seen. He'd sunk it for a three.

The boy took three swings with battered, old clubs, and birdied the most difficult hole on the course. He'd hit three perfect golf shots—without any practice swings, in his bare feet! I will tell you, with God as my witness, it was a beautiful thing to watch.

By the time the ball had dropped in the hole, the mist was rolling over us. There were wisps of it blowing toward Sweeney standing on the green. And I could no longer see back down the fairway for more than forty or fifty yards. The last thing I saw the boy do, before the mist engulfed him, was walk over to the hole, bend down and take his ball out of the hole. He seemed to be fiddling with the ball, somehow. I couldn't make out what he was doing, as it was nearly dark by then. But then he did a strange thing in that moment—he bent down and put the ball back in the hole, took his flip flops out of his back pocket, slipped into them and walked over the hill behind the green. He went right back into the woods by the downed sweetrey oak tree.

I was left there, standing in the near dark behind the bluff willow, listening to a few bullfrogs grunting from the edge of the pond. For the life of me, I couldn't figure out why he had put the ball back in the hole.

I hurried over to the green to get a look at that ball. When I took it out of the hole, I saw that he had written on the ball in black permanent marker. It read:

A solitary bird
For my companion
Upon the withered moor.
　　　　　—Senna

I keep that ball on my mantle in my room here at the home. I know he left it for me, and it's a lovely Haiku. Sweeney had known I was there watching him on the course, but it had been too long since we'd seen each other. I realized that night how much I missed him.

I miss him now, too. It was the last time I saw Yardbird Sweeney. I was told that that was the year he went traveling and didn't come back to Seawell. That was also the year they found his old, rusty beach cruiser by the base of the Pennacook Bridge.

Some of these people around Seawell think he jumped, but I'm not so sure. He wasn't really a sad or angry person, just a lonesome sort of person. Most people aren't comfortable around someone like that, they don't know what to make of a person who prefers to be alone. It scares most people, frankly.

I know that boy did not jump off that bridge. I imagine he still wanders, still looks for his place. In my heart of hearts he's camped out at some remote surfing place in Peru or South Africa, learning to listen to the tides, waiting for the far-away storms to send him some waves.

Do they even have good breakers in South Africa or Peru? I'm not even sure (*Laughs quietly to herself*).

THE GEALT, A COVERED BRIDGE

I made it through some evenings in the Gealt's
deep shade, drinking cold Pabst to fight the heat.
Swallows careened through shifting clouds of midges
above the river, along twilight's dark pleat.
I once swam beneath the bridge to check the depth
of the water with my eyes, but the mud
proved too much. So with squinched lids and held breath
I dove for the silt of the bed—through the lifeblood
of the overhanging birch and the oak knolls.
I frog-kicked downward, for what seemed like years,
but failed to touch. As I surfaced, some locals
biked between the footbridge's thick tiers.
They cursed the heat and sweated: frail, bare-chested
boys who had flown over the playing fields
for wont of freedom and quick solace wrested
from the summer's humid, repetitious yield.
I gave up on the bottom and I climbed
up the pollen-dusted boulders of the bluffs
toward the boys' swears and laughter as it chimed
thinly and shrill through the Gealt's lattice truss.
I dripped wet blots and padded on warm planks,
stenciled with long, crisscrossed shadows, to suss
out the jumping spot. The four boys stood in rank,
in line from old to young above the rain-starved
river, to wait their turn. The smallest shrank
from my question, then spoke: "Jump from where 'jump's' carved
in the wood." I watched as his delicate, white feet
gripped the plank's edge and rasped on grit and sand.
He rose and left the four, rough letters wet,
dark, sunk into the grain of the weathered wood.

—Sweeney

The Storytellers

These short biographies were completed via brief telephone interviews with each storyteller.

ERIN HAMASAKI

Age: 17 **Born:** Seawell General Hospital. **Seawell Neighborhood:** Rathmines, I grew up near the Caley School. **Current Hometown:** Seawell, but I want to go to college in Australia in a couple years, on the West Coast. I'm sick of this place. **School or Work:** Junior at Seawell High, and I'm a waitress at Bolcain Glen in Tyngsboro. School's okay, but my job sucks! **Where and when you met Sweeney:** At Seawell Beach after I ran away from home when I was just a little kid. He was getting ready to go for a surf. It was springtime. **Last time you talked to Sweeney:** I guess it was the day I met him. But I saw him surf one more time during a big day at Seawell Beach when I was older. **Where you think Sweeney is now:** He's probably surfing somewhere with cold water and big waves, like Easter Island or somewhere. He didn't jump off that bridge. No way! He got out of this stupid city and never came back.

MICHAEL JOSEPH TRABELL

Age: 11 and a half. **Born:** Kingston, New Hampshire. I lived there for a year when I was really little. I don't remember it. **Seawell Neighborhood:** Oaklands, I'm from the coolest part of Seawell. **Current Hometown:** Is this a trick question? **School or Work:** I'm in sixth grade at Oakland Elementary. Next year I go to Moody Junior High. **Where and when you met Sweeney:** I've never met him, but my dad says he was cool when they went to Seawell High. **Last time you talked to Sweeney:** Some of these questions are repeats. **Where you think Sweeney is now:** I think he's in Mexico or some jungle somewhere, but my dad thinks he jumped off that bridge because he dropped out of college or something. I don't believe him. He could be a professional bullfighter, too.

DANIEL ANDREW TRABELL

Age: It was my birthday last week. I'm 10. **Born:** In Seawell. **Seawell Neighborhood:** Oaklands, but I wish we lived in the Rathmines because my friend Tina lives out there near a cool park where the fire department makes ice for skating in the winter. They spray the senior league outfield with their hoses. Our park sucks. **Current Hometown:** Seawell, I already told you. **School or Work:** I'm in fifth grade. I get an allowance if I take out the garbage and clean up after our dog when he shits in the yard.

Where and when you met Sweeney: You already asked us about that.
Last time you talked to Sweeney: These questions are dumb. **Where do you think Sweeney is now:** He's dead, I guess. I don't know. Everybody says he jumped off that bridge over the harbor.

GERALD M. FRANCIS

Age: 71 **Born:** My parents came here from Portugal while my mother was pregnant with me. I was born in 1933 in Woburn, Mass., a few months after they arrived. **Seawell Neighborhood:** I married Walter's mother when we were both 22 years old, and we moved to South Seawell, to her neighborhood, after our honeymoon. **Current Hometown:** Oddly, I find myself still living in Seawell, Mass. I never left this place, never even traveled to Florida each year like all the other snowbirds. **School or Work:** I'm a retired firefighter. I was on the force for 30-some-odd years. **Where and when you met Sweeney:** Farannan Golf Course when he was only nine years old, I believe. **Last time you talked to Sweeney:** I suppose he was around 23 or 24 years old, around nine or ten years ago. We had a few drinks at the [Farannan] clubhouse on my birthday. That's when he gave me that poem as a gift. **Where you think Sweeney is now:** Well, I suppose he's wherever he wants to be. Whether he jumped or not, I can't say. That kid always did as he pleased, so I'll just imagine he's doing whatever he wants to do wherever that may be.

WALTER J. FRANCIS

Age: 38 **Born:** St. John's Hospital, Seawell **Seawell Neighborhood:** The Lowlands. We grew up in South Seawell, and now I live with my three daughters and my wife on 12th St. in the Lowlands—the old, marshy section of the city. **Current Hometown:** See previous. **School or Work:** I read meters for the gas company. I've been doing it for almost twenty years now. **Where and when you met Sweeney:** I met him through my father at the golf course, and he hung around with one of my second cousins when they were kids. **Last time you talked to Sweeney:** About ten years ago at Farannan with my dad. Before that? I guess it was when I was in college and Sweeney had a keg party on that old boat he lived on in the out-of-bounds area of Farannan—the one on stilts. I really haven't talked to the guy that much other than a "Hello" or "How's things?" every once in a while. **Where you think Sweeney is now:** I have no idea. I haven't thought about it much. My dad would know better than me. I hope he's laying on some deserted beach somewhere, just enjoying the sun and the surf, while we hang around like a bunch of suckers who can't wait to shovel more snow! Good for him, you know?

MIGUEL GUTIERREZ OBREGON, a.k.a. "Micky" or "Goatboy"
Age: 34. **Born:** Puerto Rico, we moved to Boston when I was four then to Seawell when I was eleven. **Seawell Neighborhood:** I grew up in the Acre, and then on the other side of the river for a while in Pentucketville, but I just bought an old cottage in Sun Valley that I'm fixing up. **Current Hometown:** Seawell. **School or Work:** I own Flintmere Treescaping and I'm Groundskeeper at Farannan. I've been running Farannan since I was a teenager, really. Timmy Danvers, the old Groundskeeper, was still around but he let me run the show most of the time. I got a guy who takes care of the Flintmere work for me, I just keep an eye on things over there and spend most of my days fixin' up this course. **Where and when you met Sweeney:** Seawell High, gym class. We were challenging each other to do crazy shit off the diving board during our two weeks of swimming for the year. We were sophomores I think. I could do one-and-a-halfs; he couldn't. He was pissed. **Last time you talked to Sweeney:** Couple nights before he disappeared. We surfed up at the points—had a good session, too—and then had some beers at McSwiggans. **Where you think Sweeney is now:** I don't know. I talked about that in the other interview, and I don't want to say anything more about it.

THOMAS SANTOS
Age: 33. **Born:** Seawell. **Seawell Neighborhood:** The Acre. **Current Hometown:** Seawell. **School or Work:** Duck Island for just about half my life. Wow, seriously. It's been almost 15 years. **Where and when you met Sweeney:** We're third cousins or somethin'. We used to play Little League together, and I guess I knew him even before that. **Last time you talked to Sweeney:** I don't know. We hung out a couple times after he got out of Darville Mental, like, the whole group of us. That was in the early '90s, but we weren't really too friendly by then. **Where you think Sweeney is now:** I hope he's surfing off of some deserted island, living in a shack in the jungle and just relaxing. I hope that's how it is, but I don't know. He might've killed himself, he might've jumped. I've seen him get pretty depressed after a bender and stuff. Who knows?

MARGARET KATHERINE TIERNEY
Age: 83. **Born:** Prince Edward Island, off the coast of Canada. **Seawell Neighborhood:** My family had moved to P.E.I. before I was born, to be

close to my mother's family, but we moved back to my father's old neighborhood, the Oaklands, when I was a toddler. **Current Hometown:** Seawell. **School or Work:** I taught third and fourth grade for thirty-five years at several schools around the city. **Where and when you met Sweeney:** Farannan Golf Course in the late '70s. **Last time you talked to Sweeney:** Well, we didn't talk but I saw him on the golf course shortly before he disappeared that fall, in 1998 I believe. **Where you think Sweeney is now:** I like to tell myself he is off gallivanting around some deserted coastline, learning about the edible and medicinal plants in some forest or jungle…well, I'll just leave it at that. I just pray the boy is okay—off by himself like that.

PETER TREVOR JOYCE, a.k.a. "The Wizzah"
Age: 32. **Born:** Seawell, Mass. **Seawell Neighborhood:** The Lowlands. If you have to live in Seawell, it might as well be in the Lowlands—God's Country, kid, no doubt about it. **Current Hometown:** Whistler, British Columbia, Canada. **School or Work:** I picked up a trade out West. I'm a unionized Ski Bum. I bartend at The Boot a couple nights a week for beer and rent money. It works for me. **Where and when you met Sweeney:** Moody Junior High, him and a bunch of other guys threw me in a Dumpster on the first day of school. They had to sacrifice a seventh grader, and why not me, right? Kind of an honor, really. **Last time you talked to Sweeney:** I guess it was almost seven or eight years ago, he drunk-dialed me from El Salvador or Honduras or somewhere. He assured me that it was really hard to get to a phone at whatever time it was down there. He rode on a Shetland pony or donkey or something, he said—like I was supposed to be proud of his effort or something. **Where you think Sweeney is now:** I don't know. It sounds stupid, but if the phone rings in the middle of the night I wake up thinking it could be him—wasted or he just got out of a Mexican Jail or something. I don't know for sure, but I think he might have killed himself because I haven't heard from him in a long time. Nobody has. Back in the day, he used to call or send a postcard to one of his old friends, no matter how long he'd been gone. The tide's so strong under the Pennacook [Bridge] they never would've found him if he had jumped. I hate to think about it, I really hate to think about it…now I'm all fuckin' sad an' shit. See, I knew I didn't want to talk about anymore of this bullshit. Edit out the tears, alright? And tell your dad I said, "What's up?"

AUDREY ELAINE GAMMENS

Age: No comment. **Born:** Galloway, MA **Seawell Neighborhood:** I just gave up an apartment that I kept during the past couple of decades in the downtown area of Seawell. **Current Hometown:** Galloway, MA. **School or Work:** I went to Galloway High, Boston University, and I've been a sportswriter since graduating. I'm currently the Sports Editor at The Seawell Times. **Where and when you met Sweeney:** I first covered him when he caught for Seawell High's baseball team. **Last time you talked to Sweeney:** He told me he had "No comment" when I tracked him down to see how the Pepperdine program was treating him. It was a few months after he had enrolled there. That was pretty much it. I couldn't find him after that. **Where do you think Sweeney is now:** He killed himself by jumping off the Pennacook Bridge in 1998, his remains are scattered throughout the ocean he seemed to love so much.

PATRICK FERGUS KIVLIN

Age: 44 **Born:** St. John's Hospital, Seawell **Seawell Neighborhood:** I grew up in the Oaklands, and I now live in Rathmines. **Current Hometown:** Seawell. **School or Work:** Environmental Consultant for The Commonwealth of Massachusetts. **Where and when you met Sweeney:** On Seawell Beach, when he was around six or seven years old. We were both down there watching waves roll in from a hurricane off the coast. The waves looked so perfect, we decided to learn how to surf together. He was just a kid, but he picked it up faster than I did. I guess I was fifteen or sixteen when we met. I was kind of a big-brother figure for him after that. **Last time you talked to Sweeney:** I'm not sure. I suppose it was a day or two before they found his bike at the base of the Pennacook. We said we'd meet for a surf, for dawn patrol, and we did. But it was blown out and we both went back to bed. **Where you think Sweeney is now:** He's somewhere in South America finishing a collection of poetry or translating the next great Chilean poet to English. I suppose that's what I'd say if I had to guess. But he still owes me five-hundred bucks for that Hynson board I lent him in 1997. So, I suppose I'll take a cut of the advance on this book, we'll buy a longboard and teach a few kids to surf this summer down on Seawell Beach. That way we can call it even between you, me, Sweeney and everybody else in Seawell who still tells stories about him to this day.

Appendix B
THE "KEMP AABERG"

Compiled by Owen Kivlin, Miguel Obregon, Thomas Santos and Patrick Kivlin

In the summer of 1986, after Sweeney's parents moved to Rhode Island, Sweeney began searching for furnished apartments in the downtown area of Seawell. He decided against living with his high school baseball coach, Jorge Mroz and his family, though Sweeney greatly appreciated the offered hospitality. He also declined an offer from my father, Patrick Kivlin. Sweeney wanted to live on his own, despite only being seventeen years of age.

Sweeney checked in with the people at the Seawell Marina to see if any old boats were up for sale at the start of the summer. He and Micky Obregon had discussed throwing a boat on a trailer, hauling it out to the woods of Farannan Golf Course behind the groundskeeping garage, winterizing it as best they could, and then Sweeney could live in it until he found a better situation. The boat was originally intended as a temporary solution.

Sweeney bought the trawler that became his Seawell home from a local fisherman known as "Gerry the Russian." The story goes that Gerry needed to get the boat out of the water, the Fish and Game Department was ready to fine him for a small fuel leak. In addition to engine trouble, the boat's hull was no longer seaworthy. It floated, and would be fine as a home on stilts, but the hull couldn't take many more poundings in the North Atlantic. Gerry the Russian didn't want to pay to haul it out of the marina, so he plugged the leak and began stalling the Fish and Game people. Around the same time, Sweeney's parents sold the family house in Seawell and were passing papers later that summer. Sweeney needed to move out of his childhood home, but he struggled to convince any landlord that he was eighteen with a reliable full-time job. Sweeney called Gerry the Russian and told him he would pay for the removal of his 32-foot fishing trawler, but he didn't have enough to buy it outright.

They apparently made a deal that involved a handshake and a whiskey sour—purchased for Gerry the Russian by an underage Sweeney at the Marina's restaurant. When I tracked him down in 2004, Gerry the Russian only offered a brief comment on the transaction. He said, "I don't remember too much about that boat. I know the guys at Fish and Game were breakin' my balls over a leak. I remember that because it was a five- or six-thousand-dollar fine if I didn't get it out of there by the end of the summer. The boat wasn't worth more than a few hundred bucks, it hadn't been seaworthy in a couple years. I just wanted to get rid of it. The kid took it off my hands, no questions asked—said he was gonna live in it or somethin' ridiculous like that. I didn't care, I just wanted it out of my sight. The whiskey was enough for me."

Gerry the Russian was pleased to hear that Sweeney had actually lived in the boat on and off for many years. "You're shittin' me? That's great," he responded.

Micky helped Sweeney tow the boat out to Farannan in the middle of a late summer night; they did some damage to the edge of the fairways and rough of the fourth, fifth and six holes, but fixed it themselves. Micky told his supervisors that some joyriding teenagers were responsible for tearing up the course. The next day, Micky claims, he and Sweeney used eight-ton jacks to take the 32-foot trawler off the trailer. Using two jacks and piles of beam ends, scavenged from construction sites, they carefully set the boat down on a pair of steel oil drums positioned at the corners of the stern, and two piles of beam ends placed beneath the bow and the under the centerpoint of the boat. They managed to perch it behind a grove of honey ash, at the base of a steep hillside covered in yew trees. They planted some fairie alder and holly saplings on the port and starboard sides hoping to keep the boat out of the wind and hidden from sight.

At the start of its new, landlocked life the boat was christened the "Kemp Aaberg," named after one of the original Malibu stylists whose silhouetted, soul-arch bottom turn appeared in the first issue of Surfer Magazine in 1960. Apparently, the christening party went so well nobody actually slept in the boat that first night. Eight or ten men and women woke up in various pits and beds of leaves on the forest floor around the boat. A small search party found the last stragglers passed out, completely naked half-on, half-off a Shamuu pool raft in the rough of the sixth hole of Farannan Golf Course.

It seems, for the most part, that Micky and Sweeney were successful. Hurricane Murgill eventually blew the Kemp Aaberg off of its improvised stilts in 1998, but not before the boat had served as Sweeney's Seawell home for nearly twelve years. It took yearly rounds of winterizing, weatherproofing, repairs and improvements, but the trawler stood up against the elements longer than anyone expected. It also was hidden well enough, after three or four years of sapling growth, to give Sweeney the solitude he desired. No one but his closest friends, and a few high school kids drinking by their fire pit in those same woods, ever visited. Not many people ventured into the out-of-bounds woods tucked in the back corner of the golf course. In fact, many of the people I interviewed for this book had heard of the Kemp Aaberg out in the woods, but few claimed they visited the boat.

Micky says he and Sweeney took the boat's leaky engine out of the engine box in the center of boat's kitchen and installed a wood stove in its place. He said the kitchen and sleeping area were spacious enough for one person: "It was only a little bit smaller than a studio apartment downtown—you know, one you'd rent for like twelve-hundred a month these days. We extended the table and the booth seating in there, and buried a generator nearby for electricity. We insulated the inside as best we could and then built a little Plexiglas enclosure over the back deck. We had the whole thing remodeled for that first winter. It was cold as hell on the deck, but the stove was almost too warm for the inside of the boat. I hung out there and played cards a lot with Sweeney back then—drinkin' beers, talkin' shit. We even had a Forty-Fives-night for a while with a bunch of guys, ya know, until Sweeney ended up at Merritt. But, yeah, the Kemp was a nice spot, and we kept it in real good shape each year. The thing lasted way longer than we thought it would! I've been thinkin' about doing it all again with another boat, same spot. It was only two or three hundred yards behind my groundskeeping garage out there. It was cool to have a place to kinda disappear to, hidden behind the earcain yews and honeycomb gorse. It was good just knowin' it was there and stuff."

In 1989, Sweeney would find likeminded surfers on the West Coast who had a surf camp on the coast of Baja called "The Boat Ranch." Tommy describes the place somewhat in detail in Chapter 5. The Boat Ranch contained fifteen or sixteen old fishing vessels, no longer seaworthy, hauled out of the Pacific and circled like a nautical wagon train at a camp in the desert on the cliffs above a surf spot. Sweeney had retreated there after he dropped out of Pepperdine. For a brief time he lived at the Boat Ranch, approximately three to four months, and he fished with the local fishermen and served as caretaker for the Ranch. The stewards of The Ranch, Lance Downs and John Stanley, let him live rent-free in the boat of his choosing while they were living and working five hours north in Southern California. From what Tommy says, John and Lance also took to Sweeney's idea of naming the boats after legendary surfers from Hawaii, Australia and California. While in Baja, Sweeney chose to live in the boat that had the best view of the surf spot from its stern. He christened that boat "The Ronnie Brosnan."

Appendix C
SᴡᴇᴇNᴇʏ 'ꜱ Fᴀᴍɪʟʏ

Compiled by Owen Kivlin, Gerald Francis, Margaret Tierney, Thomas Santos and Patrick Kivlin

I.

Despite my efforts to track Sweeney's parents down, Diane and Jonathan Sweeney refused to elaborate on their son or his whereabouts. They live together in Silver Springs, Maryland, just outside of Washington D.C, as of 2004. Mr. Sweeney has since retired from his consulting days, after closing his career working at the Pentagon. Mrs. Sweeney worked for twenty-two years as a customer representative and team manager for Nynex and its affiliates.

I spoke with Sweeney's parents separately on different dates, and Mr. Sweeney declined further comment with this brief statement: "My son made his own choices from his teen years onward. There was nothing I could do to further discipline or influence his way of thinking. I do not know where he is, and I won't speculate on his supposed suicide. If you continue to contact me I will be forced to bring this to the attention of the local authorities and my lawyer."

Mrs. Sweeney was more receptive to my phone call. She, at the very least, listened to my description of this project and seemed open to the idea. I sensed that she was almost happy for the attention paid to her son, but her overwhelming sadness at his departure from her life appeared to win out. She refused to answer any questions about Sweeney's life, and after I asked her whether or not she believed Sweeney had committed suicide or simply abandoned Seawell there was a long stretch of silence and she gently hung up the phone.

As far as I can tell—from my interviews with Thomas Santos, Patrick Kivlin, Margaret Tierney and Gerald Francis—Sweeney's parents essentially abandoned him when they left Massachusetts in 1986. It doesn't sound like they had much influence over him between 1986 and 1989. Whatever rift resulted between them, the beginnings of it seem to stem from their move away from Seawell. In 1989, Sweeney's father made an attempt to get his son back on "the right track" by sending Sweeney's cousin Tommy and Sweeney's former girlfriend Brigit Beaulieu to find his son in Baja, Mexico. Once they found Sweeney, Brigit was instructed to inform him that his father was deathly ill and wanted to see him before he passed away.

To the best of my knowledge, this all came to pass because Mrs. Sweeney had suffered a compound fracture in her lower leg that didn't heal properly and required minor surgery during the spring of

1989. Mr. Sweeney pounced on this opportunity and recruited Tommy and Brigit to the mission by bringing them to Rhode Island. He then lied to Tommy by saying that Diane Sweeney was the one who was on her deathbed and couldn't see any visitors, but wanted to patch things up with her son.

Brigit seems to have known of the deception at work, and only agreed to it in a warped effort to rekindle a relationship with Sweeney — a relationship that began and ended during their freshman year at Seawell High School. Tommy and Brigit set off for Baja together, and the rest of the story is detailed in Chapter 5.

II.

Whatever problems Sweeney had with his parents, and vice versa, their relationship appeared to come to an end with this Baja episode. Sweeney refused to speak with his parents, Brigit and Tommy after he uncovered the truth in Rhode Island. Mrs. Sweeney remained with Mr. Sweeney and, despite Tommy's speculation, it's unclear whether or not she was ever tempted to divorce him over his deceit in dealing with their son.

Sweeney's decision to quit the Pepperdine baseball team, along with the time he served at the Merritt House of Corrections, exacerbated the damaged relations with his cousin Tommy, and they were never close again.

ABOUT THE AUTHOR

Dave Robinson is from Lowell, Massachusetts. He studied Literature, the Arts and Spanish at the University of New Hampshire, Durham, and received his MFA in Poetry from San Diego State University. After eight years on the West Coast, where he worked in an insurance brokerage house, a surf shop, as a copy editor and freelance writer, as a writing instructor at SDSU, in the Museum of Contemporary Art, La Jolla, and in landscape construction, he returned to Massachusetts. He has published articles, poetry, fiction, illustrations and photos in a variety of magazines and literary journals, including *The Surfer's Path, The Surfer's Journal, Poetry International, Margie: The American Journal of Poetry, Surfer, Entelechy International, Powder, H2O* and *Renovation Journal. Sweeney on-the-Fringe* is the first in a trilogy, and Dave swears he's hard at work on the second and third books as you read this.